I0519511

AMERICA THE LATE

F.E. PRATT

America the Late
by F.E. Pratt

ISBN 978-0-692-13529-7

1st Edition

Cover art by Robert Nystrom

AMERICA THE LATE

We were in a convoy of four armored vehicles with special operations staff and regular Texas National Guard troops headed to the Texas border in Matamoros. Our objective was to go into as many communities as we could to recruit fighting men to defend Texas and establish our border. We figured it might be dodgy with as many illegals as we had down there, but that was what we were counting on for our success. Our state had been under siege for almost three months from ISIS infiltrators, Black Panthers and drug lord mercenaries. They had managed to organize the poor areas and stir them into a fighting mood. The cities were being looted. Everything was set on fire after it was cleaned out. Houston, Austin, and San Antonio were burning. We had established a security perimeter using the Beltway in Houston to keep the chaos in a designated area until we could isolate the problems and eliminate them. Dallas and Fort Worth were also in trouble, and the local police forces were being overwhelmed, but the Texas National Guard (nearly forty thousand strong) were working to build a containment area to get it under control. But forty thousand isn't enough to cover a state the size of Texas.

The Governor of Texas had called up the Texas National Guard and established a level of cooperation between them and the local police departments—and I had a big hand in that. Being a police chaplain had its benefits regarding understanding the local police mind-set. In addition, Texas was talking about pulling out of the Union again and establishing a Republic until things settled down. Our ace in the hole was to get private citizens with past military experience engaged in the fight to secure Texas. We were counting on the fact that Texas boasted the largest number of military enlistments of any state.

I was still trying to figure out how I got involved in this. We were driving, and I was looking out a window trying to collect my thoughts and determine what my role would be and how I could help get this mess straightened out. I could see on my right a faint glow of red that looked like it was coming from the Austin–San Antonio area. If I'd looked behind, I'd've seen Houston as a glow on the horizon. I looked over at the driver, Lopez, who had proven to be a talented soldier, my best friend, and the biggest asset I could ever have wanted in this endeavor.

Just as I looked to our front, a streak of light came from the right and the vehicle in front of us exploded into a giant fireball. Lopez took immediate evasive action and went left to avoid the wreckage, issuing the order for all vehicles to take defensive positions. We were under attack. The vehicle ahead of us had taken an RPG round from off the road and was burning. Our first concern was getting cover and then we needed to see if we had survivors in the front vehicle: military protocol.

As we pulled off and took up a defensive position we started taking a lot of small-arms fire. Rounds were hitting the armor and making spider-web patterns in the glass. We pulled up off to the left of the flaming vehicle, and Lopez gave the order to disperse. Our troops took up fire positions and started returning fire at the flashes we saw coming from the side of the road. Lopez was in charge. He called up two troops to go check the first vehicle and for the rest of us to set up cover fire.

Just as they left to position themselves to check out the first vehicle, we saw an RPG get launched from across the road, and it was headed for our vehicle which we were using for cover. Someone shouted "RPG, cover!", and we all dove into the ditch to try and get as much cover as we could. I was slow and the blast from the RPG lifted me off my feet and launched me in the air, my head spinning from the blast. I landed hard with my ears ringing and I couldn't figure out what was happening. My first instinct was to get on my feet but I had a burning sensation in my arm and my leg, and I was having trouble trying to get back on my feet. My body felt heavy, and even breathing was a challenge.

Lopez was there instantly and told me, "Stay still: You're hit." As Lopez worked to discover the extent of my wounds, I started fading into a weird state of fog. I was somewhat aware of things going on around me but I just could not seem to lock and load, so to speak. I kept hearing Lopez saying *Stay with me*, but I couldn't stay awake, and as I faded into blackness all I could think of was *If I die here tonight, how did I get here, and what difference have I made?* Because at the end of the day, or the end of your life, you will ask yourself if you made a difference.

CHAPTER 1:
THE WAKE-UP CALL

It was one of those perfect fall mornings on the Texas Gulf Coast. Our first legitimate cold front of the year had come through the day before yesterday, and the weather today was perfect. Early November is perfect for us islanders, because the fishing is great and the weather is awesome. The fishing is even better when a lot of the fisherman are instead trying to get their deer, since the season opens the first weekend in November. Usually the early or really strong fronts come in with a heavy dose of short-lived rain and a strong wind out of the north. I live on a small island just to the mainland side of Galveston. My house faces directly north and looks out at Jones Bay with Texas City and its refineries on my horizon. The cool fronts bring a little chop that will break on the bulkhead, and usually it's not much of a problem. But once the front gets through, things settle down, and these days are the reason I live here. The day was ramping up with a red sunrise shining off of the cirrus clouds, a very light (8 mph) wind directly from the north, and a high today of a sunny 71°.

I am 59 years old, and 40 pounds overweight, so starting the day for me is slow most days. I started today like usual: I rolled out of the sack just as the sun was coming up and staggered downstairs to get a pot of coffee going. I am not a very good morning person so I usually make a dark roast with chicory to get me wound up for the day.

After the coffee was going, I went back upstairs to shower and get ready for the trek into the office. I am a small business owner, and our office is on the north side of Houston, so I have about an hour and a half commute each way. With the ability to work electronically from anywhere, there is not much of a reason to go in to the office to talk on the phone or access e-mail. That is why I try to work from my home office as much as I can. But today I needed to be present to sign checks for accounts payable. Oh boy.

After a shower and a big cup of java to go, I kissed my wife goodbye at 7:30, told the dog "No running, jumping or biting while I'm gone," and said "Kitty, you're in charge," started the truck, and headed north to get to the office by about 9:00 AM Traffic was normal for a Monday with the usual slowdowns at NASA Road 1 and the Beltway, but after getting on Beltway 8 headed north around the east side of the belt, things moved great. I pulled in at three minutes to nine, just like I had planned

I walked into the office said my usual hellos to folks and started setting up my laptop. Shaun, our admin, always has a pot of coffee going (thank goodness!) so I could reload my travel cup and build some momentum for the day. My first action item is always to check e-mail. Nothing really stirring, but I did respond to a couple of client questions about the timing of the deliveries of some products. My usual next step is to hit my favorite news page on the web. These items were not necessarily comforting to read, but the world seemed to be escalating into a full-blown disaster, and it felt to me that our country's leadership was fine with it and was, in fact, encouraging it.

BAGHDAD *(Reuters)—The Islamic State militant group that has seized large parts of Iraq and drawn the first*

American air strikes since the end of the occupation in 2011 has warned the United States it will attack Americans "in any place" if the raids hit its militants.

The video, which shows photographs of an American who was beheaded during the US occupation of Iraq and victims of snipers, featured a statement which said in English, "We will drown all of you in your own blood.

Border Trouble

Staggering statistics that show nearly a half-million people were caught trying to enter the US illegally—and more than half were not Mexican, a number far higher than in 2013—reportedly were posted on a US government website for just a few hours last month before being taken down.

ISIS Fighters Focus on Iraq's Capital, Baghdad

Islamic State stands with al-Qaeda as one of the most dangerous jihadist groups after its gains in Syria and Iraq. Under its former name Islamic State in Iraq and the Levant (ISIL), it was formed in April 2013, growing out of al-Qaeda in Iraq (AQI).

Al Qaeda Magazine Hints of Looming Attack; Urges Bombing of Vegas, Military Targets

A new English-language Al Qaeda magazine features a how-to article on making car bombs and suggests terror targets in the United States, including casinos in Las Vegas, oil tankers and military colleges, and implies that an attack is imminent.

NO-GO Zones

The "no-go zones" in some Western nations, where law enforcement has lost control because of the influence of Islamic law, are coming to America.

As WND *reported, the government of France has identified 751* Zones Urbaines Sensibles, *or Sensitive Urban Zones, that the state does not fully control, citing Middle East foreign policy expert Daniel Pipes, director of the Middle East Forum.*

The zones are enclaves where Muslim immigrants have chosen not to assimilate, and law enforcement has lost some degree of control.

Ferguson Protester Lofts MORE ISIS Signs

Media spin feeds fear ISIS operating in US

After 30 days of nonstop rioting, during a CNN interview last night in Ferguson, Missouri more protesters held up signs declaring "ISIS is here." "How is democracy treating you guys?" ISIS militants take to social media to encourage Ferguson protesters to embrace Islamic extremism

It's funny how those headlines seem to be the focus and yet buried deeper in the site was this article:

Online posts show ISIS eyeing Mexican border, says law enforcement bulletin

EXCLUSIVE: Social media chatter shows Islamic State militants are keenly aware of the porous US-Mexico border, and are "expressing an increased interest" in crossing over to carry out a terrorist attack, according to a Texas law enforcement bulletin sent out this week.

Law enforcement and intelligence sources report the area around Anapra is dominated by the Vicente Carrillo Fuentes Cartel ("Juárez Cartel"), La Línea (the enforcement arm of the cartel) and the Barrio Azteca (a gang originally formed in the jails of El Paso). Cartel control of the Anapra area make it an extremely dangerous and hostile operating environment for Mexican Army and Federal Police operations.

According to these same sources, "coyotes" engaged in human smuggling – and working for Juárez Cartel – help move ISIS terrorists through the desert and across the border between Santa Teresa and Sunland Park, New Mexico. To the east of El Paso and Ciudad Juárez, cartel-backed "coyotes" are also smuggling ISIS terrorists through the porous border between Acala and Fort Hancock, Texas. These specific areas were targeted for exploitation by ISIS because of their understaffed municipal and county police forces, and the relative safe-havens the areas provide for the unchecked large-scale drug smuggling that was already ongoing.

Mexican intelligence sources report that ISIS intends to exploit the railways and airport facilities in the vicinity of Santa Teresa, NM (a US port-of-entry). The sources also say that ISIS has "spotters" located in the East Potrillo Mountains of New Mexico (largely managed by the Bureau of Land Management) to assist with terrorist border crossing operations. ISIS is conducting reconnaissance of regional universities; the White Sands Missile Range; government facilities in Alamogordo, NM; Ft. Bliss; and the electrical power facilities near Anapra and Chaparral, NM.

Missing Libyan Jetliners Raise Fears of Suicide Airliner Attacks on 9/11

Egypt set for military intervention as Libya spirals toward failed state

September 2, 2014 4:55 pm: Islamist militias in Libya took control of nearly a dozen commercial jetliners last month, and western intelligence agencies recently issued a warning that the jets could be used in terrorist attacks across North Africa.

Mass murder of Republican representatives

A gunman asking "Who are the Republicans here?" at a baseball practice opened fire with a long gun and a pistol in an attempt to "kill as many Republicans" as he could.

CIVIL DISTURBANCES: EMERGENCY EMPLOYMENT OF ARMY AND OTHER RESOURCES

This regulation prescribes responsibilities, policy, and guidance for the Department of the Army in planning and operations involving the use of Army resources in the control of actual or anticipated civil disturbances. Basic authority is contained in DOD Directive 3025.12, Employment of Military Resources in the Event of Civil Disturbances.

Fear of this, fear of that—I have grown accustomed to reading these kinds of things and they don't even seem to get to me much anymore. Funny how we are afraid of a group that is 40,000 strong halfway around the world, and we aren't even guarding our own border. I have become calloused to the shock factor presented by the news media and take a great deal of it not with a pinch but a tablespoon of salt. The real fear I have is focused internal to the United States and how we have been infiltrated by subversive forces that want to destroy our way of life my family has invested 400 years to build.

Sadly, it has become apparent that as Americans we have underestimated the Liberal Left. They have been successful in getting into positions of power in order to change our system of Government into a Socialist scheme. We just believed as a group of free people that the Democratic idea of change was the right thing for our republic because we were not satisfied with how things were going. Unfortunately what we didn't understand was the far Left is positioning our government to look totally incompetent so they could show the American people that Socialism was the best solution. Where they went wrong was in totally underestimating the depth and expanse of the American institution of government. So when their policies failed to change the American way of thinking they had to take more drastic measures. They then set out to prove the republican and democratic way of government is inferior, simply doing whatever it takes to make the American way of government look incompetent. And as Americans we just don't see the real scheme. Our media has become tools of the Socialist take over.

If you can see those things you can understand why no actions are taken on things like Benghazi, ISIS buildup, IRS scandals, NSA exposures, foreign policy blunders, border protection and the military: all things our government should be responsible for and competent to do. Add to that the drive to add Democrat voter base through immigration amnesty and it becomes easy to see why things have happened the way they have. When will we as Americans understand that the objective of the Socialist world is to bring down our capitalistic and republican environment and replace it with a Socialistic form of government?

I had just reopened my e-mail application when the lights surged and went really bright for a second or two and then everything went dark. Great! Just what I needed: a power outage today. After looking around the office and seeing it was the entire office I noticed something strange. My laptop went out when the lights did. That was weird since it had a battery and even if the power went out it should still work. The power supplies on laptops can handle surges too, so why did my machine die?

We are on the second floor, so I walked downstairs and outside to see what was going on. But before I could get outside a second flash lit us up, but this one was different. There it was—to my southeast was a mushroom cloud. Obviously ground based and not really massive, but plenty big enough. Oh no, I knew what that was. I have never seen an actual nuke when it popped, but there was no mistaking it. This was way too big to be a refining explosion or equipment fire; I have seen plenty of those after living around them my entire life. This was no plant incident. My guess is this was coming from the ship channel area where most of the refining companies are in Texas. Refineries—Texas City—oh no! That was only three miles from my house. My wife was there!

I pulled out my cell phone and it was dead as a hammer. This is great: no communications and no connectivity to the outside world. I stood there staring at a cloud and trying to figure out what to do next. I'd had this feeling before: It was in Manhattan on 9/11. I had a crew of nine people with me and once things started going really badly, we realized we had no communications back home or even with each other for that matter. I now know that the government will shut down all outside communications to make sure that our government responders have what they need. So even though there were several cell towers that went down on the trade towers the others were blocked so our emergency response teams could have the resources they needed. Standing there talking to each other, and having a plan for us, was all we could do.

I am no EMP expert but I do know about its effects from reading. My guess is this device in Texas City was not the culprit that caused all of the problems on the grid. It may have contributed since it was in a key area of the Texas power grid, but there must have been another event or two that coincided with the nuke in Texas City. A high-altitude nuclear detonation produces an immediate flux of gamma rays from the nuclear reactions within the device. These photons in turn produce high-energy free electrons scattering at altitudes between (roughly) 10 and 25 miles. These electrons are then trapped in the Earth's magnetic field, creating an oscillating electric current. This current gives rise to a rapidly rising radiated electromagnetic field called an electromagnetic pulse (EMP). Because the electrons are trapped essentially simultaneously, a very large electromagnetic pulse radiates through everything that can conduct the current.

If enough megatons were detonated in sub-orbit the pulse can easily span continent-sized areas, and this electromagnetic wave can affect systems on land, sea, and air. The first recorded EMP incident accompanied a high-altitude nuclear test over the South Pacific and resulted in power system failures as far away as Hawaii. A large device of only 2 megatons detonated at 200–250 miles over Kansas would affect all of the continental United States (CONUS). But to put one there it would take a space-capable country, so I wondered if it was all of the US or just selected areas. The signal from an altitude event extends to the visual horizon as seen from the burst point. So the question is did we have coordinated simultaneous attacks? As a country we have seen we can be vulnerable to this by the coordinated events of 9/11. We are so worried about being politically correct that we do not screen our airports like Israel does and we choose either to assume they are backwards or stupid, but our enemies are cunning and calculating. They also have access to our information through the web just like we do.

The effects of the EMP can cause damage to unprotected civilian and military systems that depend on or use long-line cables. Small, isolated systems not having a lot of exposure to the bigger grid tend to be unaffected. So many cables, pins, connectors, and devices are found in real hardware that computation of the progress of the EMP signal cannot be predicted, even conceptually, after the field enters a real system or a series of systems. Naturally the farther you are away from Ground Zero, the better the likelihood a small system would survive.

System failures or upsets will depend upon the details of circuit paths and interior electrical connections, and you cannot predict these beforehand. It has been proved that the region where the greatest damage can be produced is from about 1.5 to 4 miles from Ground Zero.

One of the unique features of EMP is the high late-time voltage which can be produced on long lines in the first 0.1 second. Energy pulses up and down, so late-time voltage effects how long the high voltage is sustained. This stress can produce large currents on the exterior shields of systems, and shielding against the stress is very difficult. Components sensitive to magnetic fields may have to be especially hardened. EMP effects are unique to nuclear weapons.

I know that one of the things that can make the great state of Texas strong and independent is the power grid. However, being independent can have a disadvantage if we were targeted specifically. With the right kind of weapon used on our grid, it could be crippling. A strategic strike to the heart of the grid could knock out power up and down the line over a great deal of the state. If you ever want to know where to strike our grid just look at NPR: They have it well documented. The Freedom of Information Act obviously is seen by our enemies as well.

Since I know a nuke was popped in the Texas City area, first of all, for a mile and a half (at least) nothing will be working, possibly as much as three or four miles. A more concerning thing would be the chemicals in the plants along Refinery Row, not to mention the fallout from the blast. I happen to know of one very large tank that is full of cyanide. If it gets ruptured, what happens then? I have sat on the deck and thought about that tank every time we have a cold front. At that moment, I was only sure of one thing: The refineries were struck and my house was only four miles from them. I needed to get home as fast as possible.

CHAPTER 2:
SHOCK FACTOR

I went back in the office and told the staff what I had just seen and what I thought had happened. Milton is a 20-year retired submariner so he knew what we were talking about immediately. Of course for now it was just speculation but we needed to figure out how to get everyone home as soon as possible. So what to do next? Shock is a huge problem in situations like this. Your brain just goes numb. You get frustrated because you can't think clearly, which just adds to the shock. It is self-perpetuating. Simple common-sense decisions become hard and you find yourself just waiting for someone to tell you what you need to do. That is why the military trains soldiers to react on instinct, so when the "defecation hits the rotary oscillator" they can at least fall back on training. The closest I came to serving was when I got drafted during Vietnam but failed the physical because of a sports injury, so I didn't have that basic training to create the instincts of what to do next, and even if I had, you are taught to follow orders. Right now I was the one who had to give the orders. Since I was the leader and everyone was looking at me, I had to do something.

I was in Manhattan on 9/11 with a technical team working a project so I know what happens when most of the cell towers for the city being on top of the trade centers are knocked out. The ones that were not knocked down were totally overbooked with people calling in and out, or shut down by the government to restrict communications until they knew what was happening. On 9/11 our plan was to build a strategy to get us back to our apartments where we would have a measure of safety and let things unfold for a day or two to see what our next step was going to be.

Now, I figured an EMP just fried electronics within some radius of where I was standing. No Internet, no phones: It was just the people standing around me that I could communicate with. I never realized just how electronically dependent for connection I had become, and how much I needed it.

So I quickly tried to assess our situation to try and decide what to do next. "OK, let's review. Shaun how far from here is your house?" She said six miles. "Milton, how far to yours?" He said three and a half. My situation was a little more problematic: I was currently 36 miles north of Houston, but I live in Galveston, which is a total of 76 miles from here. Our first order of business was transportation. I ran to my truck jumped in, turned the key, and... nothing. Not even a click from a dead battery. My electronics were fried too. Well, that made sense: An EMP pops everything not shielded. While able to handle the off-road and plenty of highway miles, Fords were not made to withstand the effects of a nuclear detonation. So now what?

Reassess. We had no transportation. It looked like at least one nuke went off in the refineries in Texas City and the ship channel area, and we needed to get everyone to a safe position, which is home. I went back into the office to try and collect my thoughts and build a plan. Once inside I realized I had an office full of people with the same problem: What should we do now? Guess what—I was fresh out of plans, but I didn't tell them that. We all gathered in the conference room and began to discuss what had happened and what we should do next. My admin Shaun has bad knees; she is the same age I am, so walking for her was going to be a challenge. We decided to go in two groups. I would walk Shaun home since it was in the general southerly direction, and Milton would walk the other two folks back to his house. But once I got her home, how would I get to Galveston? One step at a time is what I learned from 9/11. Do what makes sense at that time and get it done, then assess and determine your next step.

I figured I'd better see what I could take with me that was light and portable, so I returned to my truck and looked for anything I thought may be needed to make the trek. I retrieved my concealed-carry weapon, a Sig P250 in .40 caliber with a 15 round mag. I found a small but powerful flashlight, a Swiss army knife, my sunglasses, and an old cigar, and went in the office to see what supplies we had. Shaun and I collected a few bottles of water and distributed them to all the team members. We decided the best route to walk to get to her house would be down Kuykendahl and then east on FM 2920.

We all stepped out on the road where there was very little traffic and headed in different directions. Milton and his folks went west, and Shaun and I started south. I still wondered how our vehicles were disabled from a nuke in Texas City but since it was a fact they were down, I just put it in the back of my mind and started walking. We took it slow, and Shaun used her rolling thing that was a combination of a walker and a chair to cruise along. She walked on the very edge of the road and I walked just inside her on the pavement to watch for traffic if any actually came by.

We began our walk to Shaun's at 10:05 AM on the morning of November 10th, 2014. We walked directly south on Kuykendahl and then turned left, or east, on FM 2920 to head back toward her house. Moving at about 2 miles per hour we made it to Shaun's house at 3:15 PM. Not exactly a speed record but we made it without any kind of incident it was just walking, resting and the occasional stop to talk to others we ran into. The information coming from the people we ran into was sketchy and not much better than what we already knew. But we did run into one person who had relatives who lived in central Texas whose vehicle was working and decided to drive in to check on them. They heard it wasn't just one nuke: Other nukes had been detonated in the air between Houston and Austin, in Washington DC, one in the financial district of New York, and one atmospheric detonation over southern Virginia, and most of the eastern seaboard was without electricity or electronics. They said the military was responding but they were not sure who to respond to yet.

Now it definitely was starting to sound like more of a coordinated attack on the United States. Next question was: Who did it and what would happen next? In my own mind I knew who did it: It was radical Islam. Would it be an invasion or more strikes? I was betting on more strikes, and an attempt to swing our own people over to their side to fight. These groups are not the in-your-face-bring-it-on type of confrontational groups. They hit you from the side, the back, and the shadows and then run. If our government and our major financial city were taken out it would fall back on the states to deal with what happened next.

Luckily, I live in Texas and I felt better about our chances than most. However, we could be crippled because of the grid taking a hit. Invasion or not: Either way, I needed to get to a more secure and strategic position. The area I knew best was home. Most of these things I kept to myself because Shaun was stressed enough. I told her when she gets home to focus on establishing contact with relatives and for them to stay together to support each other.

Once at Shaun's house I refilled the water bottles, and added hers to my stash. She gave me a makeshift pack to carry the water and some light food supplies in. I rested for about a half an hour, and then I started my walk to Galveston. I figured it might take me two or three days to walk to Galveston. I was not dressed for a long two- or three-day walk: With nothing but cowboy boots, a shirt, a light jacket, slacks and my makeshift pack, I looked like a homeless Wall Street guy. I would figure out something as I made my way. Surely there would be someone traveling that way I could hook up with.

Once I walked down Shaun's driveway and started walking toward FM 2920, I suddenly had an overwhelming feeling that I was totally alone and might not be able to make this trip. There was no traffic. It was like Manhattan after evacuation on 9/11. I was on the second train back into the city once they opened up the 7 line and there was no traffic. No cabs, no pedestrians, nothing. It was like a science fiction movie. I have pictures of our team of nine standing in the middle of 5th Avenue and we were the only people you could see! Very creepy. I will never forget that feeling.

I didn't know what to expect on my trip, but it was just one of those things that I had to do. I have always been somewhat of a loner but I really don't like to be alone that much. All I knew for sure was I had between 65 and 70 miles to walk. These days I look at the effort and weigh it against the gain and decide if it is worth the effort. I guess that comes with age. But my desire to get home was much more dominant than my fear or my logic. I needed to get home. My wife was there and I had no way of getting a status on how she was doing if I stay here. Not to mention what she must be thinking and how worried she would be about me and what was happening. Not having resolution to those things was much worse than worrying about what might be in store in a long walk.

Going down 2920 I decided not to make the turn onto I-45 but to keep going straight to the toll road. While walking I had plenty of time to think about a route to Galveston. The toll road afforded some cover provided by trees along the side of the road as well as missing heavily populated areas. I was already getting tired and was second-guessing my ability to make the trip, but *one foot in front of the other and eyes front* was my objective. From the toll road I could see people standing outside around their businesses and that more people were coming out to see what was going on. My vision quickly began to be a 360° view of the environment around me as I neared the Beltway, and I started calculating threats and making plans to avoid them if possible. Instincts told me to avoid them, but so far nothing had actually happened to me.

The same people that loot businesses when their team wins would see this as an opportunity to begin looting. I remembered the headlines of how looting began under the cover of a protest and this started to worry me. If a thing as small as a tribute to a criminal killed by the police burned because a patron knocked over a candle, then I figured looting would start happening soon. I have never understood the mentality of "if something happens I must rob people and businesses, and destroy things." It has nothing to do with the event, but turns into a convenient excuse to take things you want from other people. It reveals the innermost part of who a person is when they take advantage of any event and use it as an excuse to take what they want. It is almost like they believe that because of this event no rules apply and now they will take what they can. Add to that a national leadership team who secretly wants to be on the street disrupting with them and you have a culture of chaos.

I tried to stay focused on the freeway so I could watch a perimeter around me of about a hundred yards in each direction as well as long-distance observation. That would act as a cushion in case things got weird. There were a lot of stalled cars on the road and some still had people wandering around them. For the most part people just looked at me as I walked by. I realized that parked and abandoned cars are great targets for looters.

Once I'd turned and made it a couple of miles on the tollway, I started getting into more populated areas, but luckily there were few businesses around the toll road, so there didn't seem to be much activity. I heard gunshots coming from my southwest. That was back toward Greenspoint, a high-crime area of North Houston. Now I was nearing the beltway so I decided to jump the wall and stay on the train tracks that ran down the middle of the toll road.

It was getting closer to dusk and I noticed more thug types coming out onto the freeway to look into abandoned cars. I also started hearing more gunfire, only this time I thought I heard a series of rapid shots and what sounded like an exchange of fire.

The thugs were looking for anything left inside cars that they might steal. Just as I got to the beltway things started to get weird. Three young black guys were breaking into a stalled car on the northbound side of the toll way. One of the thugs waved a gun in the driver's direction and told her to leave. The owner stood back about a hundred feet and watched like she didn't know what to do and seemed powerless to do anything about it. My fear was what would happen to the owner once they had been through the car. I hoped she would turn and run away, but shock had her and she was frozen in place.

That was when I started to feel vulnerable. I tried to stay as far away from the activity as I could, but I knew it was inevitable I would have an encounter, and it could be soon. I unsnapped the strap on my carry weapon. It was just a matter of time before they turned on the owner, so I had to go over there. She was moving back, watching one of the things she had worked hard for get mauled and taken from her, scared and frustrated and feeling violated.

My sense of exposure began to really come online. I found myself trying to keep a handle on my full 360° perimeter, basically keeping my head on a swivel. But at the same time a sense of justice was starting to overwhelm me. As I slowed for a good look at the situation, the three noticed me but kept on with their activities. It reminded me of dreams I used to have where I was at school and realized I was naked. How did I get here like this? What do I do now?

After taking their time looking through the car and picking up a few small things the group of three started a slow saunter toward me. I tried to act unfazed and kept walking like I had someplace to be. I figured if they were focused on me it might give the girl a chance to get away. I started looking around by shifting my eyes without moving my head much to see if I had any options. I moved up the tracks until I had a place I could jump the wall and have a car for cover. I kept walking and they kept closing. I know you never pull a weapon unless you have full intent of using it, so my weapon stayed in the holster for the time being. I checked my surroundings and saw a stalled car in the inside lane about forty feet from me. I figured I could get there before they did and still have about a fifteen-foot cushion so I picked up my pace and headed for the vehicle.

I got to the driver's side of the car and, as expected, they were about fifteen to twenty feet from me. Then one of them pulled a pistol out and held it in that crazy sideways gangster style waving it at me saying "What you doin' out here?" I couldn't help but notice the barrel was pointed to my right because he was a lot more infatuated by the look he presented than the actual usefulness of the weapon. That was for looks and not reality; this made an impression on me. This was a clear weakness and I felt a little better if things got really bad. The one next to him pulled back his shirt and he had a gun in his pants. They thought that by showing me some firepower and looking threatening they could make me run away or give them what they wanted.

I reached the car I was headed for and stopped by the hood so the car would give me cover if I needed it and said "Look, I am just trying to get home. I don't want any trouble." They slowly spread out to block my route moving forward. I noticed the car owner had retreated to a safe distance but was still watching. The self-designated spokesman said "Well, you are going to have trouble, so why don't you give us your wallet and what's in that sack?" I knew this was going to get ugly really quick, because that would not happen.

My pulse was racing. Everything in me said this was going to be bad. I said "OK, hang on. Let me get everything out for you. I don't want any trouble." I reached both hands around behind me. With my left hand I started moving the pack, and with the other I drew my .40. Then someone said "That isn't going to happen" out loud. It was me! I don't know where that came from. I dropped down behind the car and fired 1, 2... 3, 4... 5, 6, I double-tapped all three. From 15 feet that was not hard to do. They were all show and no dough, as we say in Texas. Just like I was taught in tactical training, *don't think, drop and shoot if your life is in danger*. The key is to know when your instincts tell you now is the time. All three went down. Two didn't move much, the third was struggling some. I walked over to the gangster weapon waiver and took his weapon. A Beretta knockoff Taurus 9mm—a cheap version but it looked like it would shoot. I used his weapon to put one in the forehead of the one still moving. It did shoot, not real sweet but it would shoot. I hate the Barettaknock offs: They are really uncomfortable in my hand. But it had a nice shiny silver nickel finish.

Then I quickly frisked each of them for anything I could use. The one who flashed me his weapon had another 9mm Smith & Wesson, so I kept the better of the two 9s, which was the S&W. I collected all the ammunition from both, as well as confiscating a rather large knife from the third, and I tucked the Smith 9mm in my belt in back and started walking and looked around for the car owner. 9s...? Seriously, they are not for knock-down power. They were made to give a lot of firepower to people but volume of shots may not compensate for the direct hit of a high-caliber weapon and the stopping power. That is why in WWII the US Army decided to go with .45 calibers in the South Pacific instead of .38s. The Japanese were just too hard to bring down so a bigger grained bullet at a larger caliber was needed. Now I had just seven rounds in my .40 so I intended to use the 9mm for confrontations as needed. It had a full fifteen rounds in the clip. My .40 was for my personal protection if it came to that.

I walked over and handed the woman the nickel finish 9 and a full clip. I showed her how to use the safeties and asked her where she lived. Luckily, she lived north of our position and I told her I'd just come from there, and for her to stick to the road and get there as fast as possible. She picked up her purse and a couple of things like her glasses out of the car, then she said Thank You and started walking. I was a little concerned she would make it OK but I knew the area was clear and I still had a long way to go. I wasn't even a quarter of the way yet.

To say my adrenaline was pumping was an understatement, so my pace quickened for about a half a mile or so. Then I got the shakes. Then I barfed on the railroad tracks. The adrenaline was wearing off and what I had just done was really starting to come back on me. Did I need to shoot? Could I have talked my way out of it? I doubt it. I have never fired a weapon at a human before. I have been in some bad situations, but never one where a gun was waved at me. Little did I know that event would only be the start of a trail of hard and ugly things I would have to do.

CHAPTER 3:
JUST KEEP WALKING

I turned east on the beltway. I drove this road every day and I knew there was a lot of cover once I cleared Highway 59 headed east, so I tried to get there as fast as possible. My feet were killing me. Boots and jeans are not the best hiking attire.

I could hear much heavier gunfire from behind me so my only objective was to put distance between me and those guns. That much gunfire meant a small war was breaking out and I wanted some distance from it. The worst spot I figured would be the three miles between where I was now and getting over the 59 overpass. There were a few convenience stores just before 59 that in my mind would be targets for looters, so I tried to stay on the other side of the barrier so it would be harder to spot me and I could drop down for cover if I needed to. Just then I heard three shots ahead of me. Two shots were from a pistol and one from a shotgun. I have hunted enough birds in my lifetime to know what a shotgun sounds like versus a pistol. I stayed low and kept moving as fast as I could.

As I suspected, there was a group of about six looting the convenience store on the north side of the Beltway at Vickery. I wanted to stay away from those kinds of numbers so I got real low and moved on east. I almost made it past them when I was surprised by someone coming from the south side onto the belt. I stopped and waited to see what they were going to do. At first the person just stood and looked at me trying to see for sure what I was. It was dusk and the sun was behind me and since I stopped moving it was hard to tell. I knew I had a problem when he looked back and said something to someone else just coming onto the road surface. Then I knew I had to get some distance between me and the six at the store to try and limit the numbers I would have to engage at one time. The two plus another six could prove fatal. I stood up and walked straight ahead just like I was supposed to be there. I almost made it by them before one of them said "Hey, stop!" — spoken as though they were the kings of the area and I needed to pay attention to them.

I pulled the 9 from my back and held it close to my side because I knew they would have trouble seeing it. I kept walking like I was not involved, but they were not satisfied with that and started to create an angle to cut me off. I grabbed the flashlight in my left hand and held the 9 in my right. As they got close I told them I didn't want any trouble; I was just trying to get home. (Where have I said that before?) They kept walking to me. Then I heard it again, "I said: What you doin' here?" so then I stopped. I said "Well, you asked me to stop, but I decided I wasn't going to." I turned to face them both and they closed to within about ten feet or so. I felt something inside of me that scared me; I felt like it didn't matter what happened: I was not going to be intimidated by these clowns. One stepped toward me (now nine feet) and said "You don't belong here, homie." Later I asked myself, *what is a homie? It sounds like I am from here yet he told me I didn't belong: curious.* I said "I know, but I have to pass through. Just let me go." One more step by him, and I would have to end this threat. Then he shifted a little sideways and the other one drew to the same nine-foot range. When he reached in the front of his pants like he was going to pull a weapon I turned on the flashlight directly into his face and double-tapped both of them: 1, 2... 3, 4. They went down. Death by firearm is not as clean as it looks in the movies. They struggled for a minute or so, then they went still.

Checking his pants... Yep, there it was: another 9mm—another cheap knock off! His partner only had a locking-blade knife, another big one. I took the ammo and the knife and tossed the gun when I reached the pond just the other side of 59. Body count was starting to pile up and I was the one doing the piling. So far I had killed five guys who just were not satisfied until we had a conflict. All were young black men. Total weapons retrieved: three pistols and two knives. But now I had two full clips of 9mm ammo and a couple of knives.

This time, I didn't have the shakes like before. Instead I just felt heavy, like I was pushing through soft ground. Once I made another half mile, the woods started on the south side of the belt. I moved to the edge of them so I would have cover available whenever I needed it. I turned in the woods and sat down to get a second wind and to rethink my plan. I could see down the belt for a couple of miles and could see back to the overpass on 59. This was enough cover to allow me time to hide if I needed and some time to observe what was going on around me.

I dozed off and woke up to the sound of heavy trucks on the belt. Looking at my watch, I saw I had been asleep for almost an hour and a half. It was totally dark now. The trucks were coming from behind me and just going over the 59 overpass. I ducked in behind the trees to see what the traffic was. Military. Looked like the National Guard. Three trucks, one was a Humvee with an M60 on top, and two were troop carriers moving slow. Uh oh, this thing must be getting ugly. My guess is they were patrolling a perimeter and establishing a base of operations.

I could still hear gunfire and it sounded like mixed skirmishes coming from behind me. Whoa! What was that? That was an explosion! I could see the backlight from a fireball; it looked like it was about eight to ten miles from where I was. It came from my south and east, which was toward the plants along the Deer Park and Pasadena refinery area.

What was going on? I started to wonder what if the entire country was paralyzed without electricity or transportation what would happen. It has always been suspected that a terror group would hit soft targets first but what if it was coordinated enough to do both: take out communications and electricity, and then be completely open to hit soft targets? Then to assimilate the country they would start in the poor sections of the city and would encourage and coordinate looting, and then police would be called in. At first the police would try to treat it as riot control and take a defensive posture. Much like what happened in New Orleans after Katrina. Once the real terror instigators came in, then things would begin to escalate. Look at how it went down in Mississippi.

Because of our border not being controlled and hundreds of thousands of people flooding the southern states, we have now opened the doors to not only immigrant workers looking for a break but sleeper cells from terrorists. Our agents on the border were so overwhelmed with children and the human crises, plenty of other traffic was coming over unnoticed. Our Border Patrol continues to have a reduced budget and is told to release the illegal immigrants. Now with a No Deport order we just said you are welcome: Send us your poor, your downtrodden and your terrorists!

Once here and implanted in the poor neighborhoods terrorists would target the poor neighborhoods where they could pass as poor minorities. And to think we created this scenario ourselves because one group of politicians wanted to ensure the vote count for themselves. Even more sinister: What if that party was actually trying to repress the vote of conservatives and they were willing to break the law to do it? That idea scares me. As does the idea our leadership just hated the

Republic and wanted a Socialist government and would do anything to destroy the country to remake it in the shape of a Marxist regime.

Once in the neighborhoods the terrorists would be in perfect position to be instigators against the system. If they began to promote their radical ways during a time of high frustration they could make some headway. It is estimated that several thousand western fighters are in ISIS. To begin an uprising internally against us, using our own people, is a great tactic. So far our government has not decided to retract the citizenship of those Americans, so they could come back anytime.

In Mississippi they actually started showing ISIS flags during the riots. In fact, if I was a terrorist, my plan would be to turn all of the minority groups against the system to take it to The Man. Looking at history, Al Qaeda has established their reign in areas where there is extreme poverty and the poor are looking for something to give them hope. ISIS tells them that destroying The Man gives hope. We used the same tactic when the Afghans were fighting the Russians. Our own special forces training is working against us: We taught the worst of them how to fight the government in charge.

Once it got to the point the police could no longer keep peace they would have to withdraw and set a perimeter. Then if things continued to escalate, the National Guard would be brought in. This would only further incite the crowd and tensions would again escalate. If this was happening in every major city in the US the only solution would be Martial Law. If I were trying to take over a country as big as the US, it would be smarter to try to target some strategic areas and build a base to work from rather than everywhere at once. However, chaos in multiple locations would be a great distraction.

Ok, if it has become this bad, could it have happened quickly? Is there something I am missing? Why the quick escalation of the National Guard? Here came another group of trucks, this time with five vehicles.

Three more transports and two more armored vehicles. These were moving faster.

What if this was a planned and coordinated attack, the sleeper cells having forewarning of the timing and being prepared to escalate quickly knowing that they would get support from more sleeper cells as they were activated? It would take a plan that would know where the biggest impacts would be and what actions the cells should take. If the enemy had been ingrained in our society long enough they would know us and how we would react. If this was planned in the right areas, and the local government had been made dysfunctional, then terrorists could recruit entire neighborhoods as troops. These would quickly overrun police, and by the time the National Guard got there the areas would be established for the base of an Islamist state within the continental United States. Add to this what we have been seeing lately with the public destruction of the integrity of the police, people were being trained to distrust them and it is the perfect scenario for a takeover.

Once implanted, rooting them out would mean the killing of US citizens. Politically, this is a problem... and since our country seems to run on politics and not ethics and morals, this could fester for a long time. By removing morals and efforts now the problem is much deeper. To remove it requires a soul change, or a form of genocide only seen in directorships. This effort alone would remove the US from the international arena and force us to focus on ourselves. Without US intervention in most areas of the world the terrorists would have free rein. As we have seen from our most recent policies where ISIS was allowed to grow with financing rivalling most countries and before you know it, Islam would run the rest of the free world and have footholds in major US cities.

Sadly, it looks like the minorities and poor have been trained for a revolution for a very long time. We have dumbed our society down with the help of outside forces that created a watered-down education system. We have half of our country on welfare and government support so they are totally depending on handouts. These groups are almost totally in the large cities where the aptitude is toward getting support from the government instead of attaining self-reliance. The large cities are perfect strongholds for our enemy and will give them the leverage and the cover they need to control the country.

In our welfare state the not-so-well-off have been trained to believe they are owed support and it is the responsibility of the government to take care of them. We have trained them through recent history to expect provision from the government as well as a continuous teaching of how Socialism is the nirvana for all societies. What a great strategy by our enemy: Break down the basic principles of what makes America great and turn the population into a group of ill-informed masses that are owed things they didn't work to achieve, and we have the basis for what is happening now. Cloud all of that with a great deal of discomfort and here we are.

With the liberal takeover of our media you have the perfect platform for making sure only one side of the story gets out. The mainstream media has had an agenda to get the Left in office for many years, pounding and pounding points that they think will help get liberals elected to the point that the constituents become totally enraged. Then like in Iraq when the pullout of our military—the only stabilizing centric force—occurs, it destabilizes the country and backfires when another terror group comes in to fill the void. When the terrorists come in and behead and murder thousands, and military action is required, all the talk of no more war and baby killing gets in the way when you really need to fight.

Texas has not been very popular with the current liberal regime so if we were being overrun it would not get the attention a more liberal state like California would get. If thousands and thousands of people, drugs and guns could cross the borders, terrorists could provide guns in the neighborhoods to arm them. *Now we have a problem, and getting out of this mess will cost a lot of lives*. All I have to discern this with is the presence of the military in one day's time and the observations I have seen in my 59 years. Somebody knows more than I do.

I am just trying to get to Galveston.

CHAPTER 4:
I NEVER EXPECTED THIS!

OK, it's time to start moving.

I got up and realized my feet were really sore and my leg muscles were stiff, but after I got up and started moving it smoothed out for me. I stayed off the main belt and on the feeder where I could run into the woods if I needed to. I was really thirsty so I downed a bottle of water I brought with me from Shaun's. *Shaun's house, man! How long ago was I with them?* Seemed like forever, but it was only 28 hours ago. Now I was past Wilson Road, and staying close to the woods made me feel better and I hadn't had any encounters.

I passed through a toll booth station area and realized I was coming up on some subdivisions that I thought would be OK, but I still needed a plan to avoid conflict: I would move back and forth across the belt, using the woods as cover. In addition I would use the trees planted along the median as cover too. Ahead I could see that there was some activity and realized this was near an area of stores that could be targets for looting. Shots fired! Lots of shots, some automatic weapons. That was new, and took things to a whole new level. I see the first three military vehicles on site at the group of stores. They were deployed and engaged in a fire fight with a scattered group that seemed to be firing from three different locations. I could tell from the muzzle flashes where the groups were located.

I knew the military guys would have a security perimeter with people watching their backs, so I decided to sit and watch for a while. There was intense fighting for about three minutes and then total silence. *Looks like the US military won. Imagine that.* I decided to start slowly walking but to walk directly down the middle of the belt so there would be no reason to think I was up to something. I made it about a hundred yards and got a "Stop! US Army," so I did what any clear-headed American would do: I stopped and threw my hands up in the air and waved them around.

Two soldiers approached me and told me to put my hands behind my head. As they got closer I told them I was armed and licensed to carry, and I was trying to get home to Galveston. They said "Stay still" and searched me. Finding my .40 and the 9 and the two knives they said "You really were armed."

I said "Yes sir, and I just walked here from the Woodlands." The lead soldier asked, "The Woodlands? Where is that?" I said 27 miles north of Houston. One soldier asked "Where are you headed"? "To Galveston," I said, "I live there. Can you tell me what is going on? I really need to get to my wife in Galveston." The soldier said "Well, sir, I have some bad news for you. Most of Galveston was wiped out either by fallout or by toxins released from the chemical plants."

"Soldier do you have an officer I can talk to? I am on your side and I am just trying to get home." The soldier called out "Sarge!" and a typical stereotypical wide at the top and narrow at the waist soldier walked over. (I was wide at the top and the bottom, making a perfect square.)

"What do you want corporal?"

"Sir, this man requested to speak with you."

The Sergeant said "Yes sir, what is your question"?

"Sergeant, I have been walking for over 28 hours now trying to get home. I believe my wife is at our house on Tiki Island, a small island just north of Galveston. I have been walking since yesterday morning to get home. I am sure she is worried sick about me and I am worried about her, so I need to get there. I have not had any communications with anyone and I don't know what is going on, can you please fill me in so I know what is happening?"

The Sergeant said "You can stand up, Sir." As I stood up, he said "Sir, a lot has happened. Here is what I can tell you: First of all, the government of the United States of America has declared Martial Law. You are being retained by the Texas Army Reserve Forces. There is a curfew for all citizens and you are in violation of that curfew. Second, we believe the US was attacked by a foreign enemy and you could potentially be a combatant."

"Can you give me some more detail on what has happened?"

"A foreign force detonated five nuclear devices as well as multiple IEDs in populated areas. Nukes were detonated in Texas City, DC, Manhattan, Boston and one airburst between Houston and Austin. Additionally, car bombs have been detonated in almost every major city across the southern and eastern part of the country. I asked, "how did the local nukes have this much effect?" He said the airburst was at about thirty thousand feet, and the others were ground based.

I thought, *the atmosphere!* And I asked if it had been detonated on a plane over the areas. "Yes, Sir. Why would you ask that?" I said "It would be impossible to cover the area they needed to cover if it wasn't from the air. Missiles would be detected but pre-arranged flights would be OK, according to the FAA. That way you get line of sight coverage by popping them in the air." He said "You seem to know a lot about this kind of stuff." I said it was mostly from reading and having a lot of time to think while I was walking. I asked him if he knew if it was one of the airliners that ISIS captured. He said he didn't have that information.

I said "Sergeant, I was thinking this is probably a coordinated attack on our country and that there was a plan to pop all of the nukes at the same time and strategically knock out certain areas and blow the electric grid. In addition, I believe some of the secondary explosions I am hearing are from targeted areas being hit by terrorists." He said, Go on. I said "My bet is we now have Islamic terrorists setting up strongholds in poor areas of the major cities. They are packing military arms and my bet is they were smuggled in from Mexico. I figure the cartels have been working with the Islamic groups for several years to get them in here. In addition you are finding foreign fighters in the groups and they came over the border from Islamic countries during the open borders times. Am I right so far?"

"It's possible."

"OK, if that is possible let's just say that the terrorists built cells in the poor areas of the cities and they have incited them to revolt against the government by influencing the thought patterns to believe they were being wronged by our society. Now they are encouraging them to establish an Islamic state and take what they need from the establishment who has been cheating them for years. How am I doing so far?"

"Keep going."

"Now you guys are here because the police cannot control this and the US Government declared Martial Law." He said "Almost correct . The National Guard is here on orders from the state. So far, US martial law has not been declared across the country."

I asked him how much of our government was still intact. He said mostly the state governments, the military command mostly is based on state control and a few contributions from the national government. Austin has moved their base of operations to another city and is setting up command and control for emergency management now. "Who is calling the shots?" I asked. He said he was getting orders from his commanders within the state of Texas, and as for where they were getting their commands, he wasn't sure.

Mostly to myself but out loud I said, we are at war. He said "It looks that way. Only this time it is on our own soil." He asked me what I had seen in my walk from the north side of town. I told him about the areas I encountered looting and the types of people I was running into. I didn't mention the fire fights because I wasn't sure how that would go. I told him where the majority of gunfire was coming from and the nature of the fire. It mostly sounded like small arms like pistols and shotguns but there was an occasional full auto too.

I asked him what his plan was for me. He said "Well, I really don't have one." I asked him how long he was going to be in this area and he said "We are doing some recon to make sure the area is clear, and then we will continue moving south on the belt. I said I understand, we all have a lot of information to gather. I asked if I could rest a little bit close by because it was the first time in a couple of days or so I felt somewhat safe. He said that was fine, but to stay within the perimeter so nobody shot me. I piled up close to the barrier wall on the belt with my back to it and facing where the troops were deployed. I was asleep in seconds.

I don't know how long I was asleep but woke up hearing someone shout "RPG!" and then a loud explosion. When I opened my eyes, I could see that the first troop transport vehicle about a hundred yards from me was burning. Soldiers started barking commands and people started moving to cover positions. Now fire was coming from the tree line again and they were splattering bullets all over our location. I have been downrange and know what a bullet sounds like going over; they seemed to be coming from everywhere.

I suddenly felt really exposed and defenseless, so I got up and moved really low to a stalled vehicle for cover. Two soldiers ran by me to take up a position to the right of us, I reached for my weapon but remembered they had taken them from me. I could see the Sergeant about fifty yards from me and ducked down and started moving toward him. He saw me coming and told me to get back to the vehicle. I yelled back "I can fight! And I am not sure the vehicles are where I want to be right now. Don't leave me here unarmed." He paused and then moved toward me. "Your weapons are in the third truck. Don't shoot any of my guys."

"I can help cover the rear but I will need a long gun," I said. He moved with me to the vehicle and found my pistols and then handed me an AR with a vest holding four clips. He asked me if I knew how to use it. I said "You bet! I have an AR at home and use it to hunt pigs and deer all the time. Plus the SWAT team lets me shoot their stuff for fun."

I took a position on the other side of the concrete barrier that was the median. I hugged the wall and pointed my weapon back down the highway. I occasionally peeked up to look at the other side of the road when I could.

Then at about seventy-five yards or so I thought I saw a figure crouched low and moving across the road and then he jumped the barrier. Now he was on my side of the road. That really started my heart racing. I always thought that seeing a deer got the adrenaline working, but this was off the charts. Then a second came across. Now I officially had buck fever. I got back into a flattened position against the wall and pointed my rifle down the road. There was a slight curve in the road and if they stayed against the barrier I would see them at about 40 yards. I needed to wait until I could see both of them before I started firing. Because unlike a deer these guys shoot back.

The level of fire around me was definitely picking up, but now it seemed to be mostly coming from the soldiers returning fire at the tree line. A soldier got in the vehicle that had the mounted M60 and started firing at muzzle flashes. From every fourth round of the tracers I could see he was on point and he was at least keeping them low to the ground or possibly killing some. I heard an occasional yell so I figured somebody was taking rounds. Then, there the first one was, forty yards and crawling along the wall. He was so preoccupied with getting up behind the trucks he wasn't looking for shapes laying down against the barrier. Then I could just make out the second guy coming around the curve. I put my sights on the first one and let go two three round bursts. Then I elevated a little and did two more three round bursts. The first guy was totally clobbered; the second guy took a couple too and was screaming. I got up on my knees and sent three more into him to end it.

I wasn't ready to crawl over to check out the two but I kept my rifle on them until I knew there was no movement. Then I peeked over the wall to see how the fight was going and to make sure there wasn't anyone else crossing the road. Things had settled down a lot. I guessed that the M60 had something to do with that. I waited until I saw some troops begin to gather at the first vehicle, which by now was a total loss. Then I jumped the wall and moved toward the group of soldiers. I raised my hands and said "Hey guys, it's me." I figured they didn't know me well enough to recognize me, and I didn't want any holes in the only shirt I had.

As I walked up the Sergeant asked me if that was me shooting behind the barrier, I said "Yep, there were two guys trying to flank us. They are not a problem now." He looked at me and even though it was dark I could see a grin on him that almost showed some teeth. He said good job, and asked if I was hit anywhere. "No," I said. "I may have to change my shorts, though. Who are these guys?" The Sergeant said "My intel says they are affiliated with ISIS: You were right on your guesses. They have been recruiting here for some time and have been smuggling weapons into the US waiting for a coordinated attack on US soil. They figure the inner cities are easy to get on their side after knocking out all power and communications. Now they are trying to establish a perimeter to keep the military from coming in while they are setting up shop."

I asked "Do you think most of the people shooting at us tonight were local and have been recruited by Islamic terrorists?"

"No doubt about it. We found several bodies, three young black men, one Hispanic with gang tattoos. We need to go look at the two you have down to see what they are as well. We have known that the cartels were working with ISIS to smuggle in people and arms, but the open border policies recently by our government prevented us from really doing what we needed to do to stop it."

"So, then, your team must be a recon group to assess the situation?"

"Exactly, and to add some support if needed to law enforcement. There are teams all around the Beltway and some are taking really heavy fire. The ones on the southwest side of town near 59 are getting pounded as are the ones at the North freeway and the belt. We are heeded south now to assess the I-45 area at the Beltway." I asked if they would be going around the belt to get there and he nodded. I asked if I could ride to the Highway 3 exit just before I-45. "I think I have proven I can be OK in a fight too."

He looked at me and paused, then said "You are a civilian. I don't know if I can do that."

"Sergeant, look at who we just had a firefight with, there are no civilians anymore!" He paused again and asked me what my name was, I told him Terrell, Will Terrell. He looked at a trooper standing by me and said "Soldier, get this man a helmet and a flak jacket." Then he told me to get in the transport vehicle. I said "You wouldn't happen to have some different boots would you?" and showed him my cowboy boots, he grinned and said "No, sir. Sorry about that."

While I was getting geared up two soldiers got in the transport and said "Of the two you took out one was Hispanic, had gang tats. The other was Middle Eastern. Man, you dropped the hammer on those guys: It was hard to tell what they looked like. They were carrying AKs and had vests with extra clips so they have been outfitted to fight."

They threw the weapons they had collected from all of the casualties along with the ammo in the back of the truck. One of the troops said to me "Good shooting."

"Thanks, but that was just survival instincts that said keep shooting till the danger is gone."

One said "You can cover my back any day." Man, was I proud to be with these guys! These guys were best of our best and they were trying to save our country on our own soil. I wondered if ISIS knew what kind of sleeping dragon they had wakened. These were not politicians, these were soldiers who had families in this country, and they were really pissed.

I asked what the black guys were wearing. They said one had a black uniform and insignia that looked like the Black Panthers. Now we had clear proof the cartels and fringe radical groups had been working with ISIS to get in the country. And they were pulling together the cartel and black radicals to fight against us.

Once we were underway, the trip was a lot less exciting. No shooting, but the gunner on the M60 stayed on point checking the perimeters as we motored down the beltway. I suddenly realized I hadn't eaten anything for two days, I asked the guys in the transport if they had anything to eat they said "No, just these MREs." "What's an MRE?" "Meals Ready to Eat, or Mostly Recycled Excrement." One of the guys pitched me one. I opened it to find a little peanut butter, some crackers and a pack of something that must have been potted meat. It felt weird but because I used to eat this when I was a kid I was OK with eating it. I drank a bottle of water and asked for another. Once I finished the potted meat, water, crackers, and peanut butter, I leaned back against the wall and closed my eyes.

CHAPTER 5:
A CHANGE IN PLANS

I woke up when I heard the sound of rifles being loaded. My hosts told me to refresh my clips and to lock and load. The vehicles stopped, I asked what was going on. A soldier said "Stay here while we check it out." Then a soldier come to the back of the vehicle and said "Terrell, Sarge needs to see you." I climbed out of the transport and moved to the lead vehicle. I could finally read the name on his uniform it said Kyle.

Sergeant Kyle said "Terrell you won't be going to Galveston today. It's still a hot zone." I asked what that meant and he said "It is compartmentalized and no one goes in or out. There is still too much radiation and there were some chemical leaks from the refineries as well. So you have a choice: I can let you out here, or you can stay with us for a day or two."

I raised my right hand and said "Swear me in." He grinned again and said "OK, but don't you go and get yourself killed on my watch."

I told him I was just thinking the same thing.

Once back in the transport we were rolling again. I could hear radio chatter up front but couldn't really tell what was going on. But then the level of intensity from the person on the other end of the radio picked up, and I heard gunfire in the background. The speed of the trucks picked up. The corporal looked around and said to all of us "We are going into a live fire zone. Get out, stay low and look for cover immediately. Deploy in cover for an exit formation and *DO NOT STAND AROUND!* Stay close enough to hear my commands and set up your field of fire so you have a 45° area you handle and have part of the area for your buddy on each side. Terrell, you do know what a 45° area is, right?" I said "Yes sir. I did barely manage to get through high school."

Kyle said "Don't let your position be overrun: They will execute you if you surrender, and if the line breaks we all die here tonight—and nobody will die on my watch." Then he looked directly at me and said "Terrell, stay on my 6 no matter what." I said "You can count on that."

He said "You do know what my 6 means, right?"

I said "I will crawl right up in your butt crack, Corporal." I heard a couple of snickers from the other guys and he nodded and said "Good."

Just for a second I asked myself, *What are you doing?* Then I figured I might as well be with guys who could fight together rather than be out there all by myself. Either way I would have to fight, so this way I'd stand a chance. After all, what chance did an old fat guy have alone?

They started rolling out of the truck, guys dispersed in a 180° pattern with a few covering the rear, and the Corporal waited until they were out, then he stepped out and did a quick look to make sure everyone was where they needed to be and said "OK, follow me." I did what I was told.

I could see another group of vehicles up the road about 200 yards from us. They were on point and suddenly everyone was engaged. It seemed like firing from the right side of the road was coming from everywhere. What were maybe eight or ten bad guys before seemed like twenty or thirty now. I ran with the Corporal to some trees down and to the right and we took cover as best we could. Unlike what you see in the movies, trees do not offer much cover unless they are really big. They will hide you and make you a harder target, but bullets can go through the smaller ones.

The M60s on the vehicles opened up. Now there were two of them putting lead downrange. For about thirty seconds the return fire was intense, both groups exchanging fire. Then some explosions: looked like grenades being thrown back and forth. Our end was pretty quiet but I could see the lines of fire were rotating our way and away from the heavy machine guns. That's not good but it also meant the enemy was running away. I tried to hide behind a four inch oak tree but I knew that wouldn't work well since my girth was about 48 inches. Then, muzzle flashes came from directly in front of us but aimed back toward the group to our left. The corporal said "OK, on my signal you and I will put some rounds into the spot where the flashes came from." I said OK: Not much reason to say anything else.

He said "Now!" and we both put three bursts into the spot and the muzzle flashes stopped. We swept back left and put a few bursts into the trees farther to our left. Once the bad guys knew they could not move to their left, that it was covered, they started to move back. One thing I had already noticed is they don't like a straight-up fight: They hit you in the cheapest, most deliberate, way they can and then withdraw. Seems like their courage comes when you are unarmed or badly outnumbered then they like to show you who is in charge. Beheading of a tied up person seems to be one of their favorite things to do for the camera, but if you are shooting back they run and duck and cover. No Banzai charges from these guys. They thought they may have had the advantage until our group showed up. We just added another M60 and thirteen more good guys.

And almost as quick as it started it was over. When there was no fire from the trees then there was no return fire from us. I looked at the Corporal and asked "Are you guys under Return Fire Only orders?"

"Yes, sir."

"When do you think that will that change?" He said "When it's on our soil, I doubt that it will."

"Then that means you guys will always get fired on first and that means more casualties. Based on the last twenty years or so I would say that has become your standard operating mode." He looked at me and said that went with the job.

"Corporal, can I ask your name? I would at least like to know the name of the man I could die with tonight."

"Walters, Jim Walters."

"What group are you guys with?"

"36th division, based in Texas."

"No kidding? My dad was in the 36th during WWII. He went from North Africa to Belgium with the 142nd Battalion. He made the first beach landing of the European campaign in Italy. He got a Purple Heart, a Bronze Star, and a Silver Star. Must have been a pretty bad old turd, but he wouldn't talk about it to me."

Corporal Walters said "I can understand that. Those guys went through some really deep stuff. The 36th had one of the highest casualty rates in the war."

We were quiet for a minute or two and then I asked him "Do we go check things out now?"

"We need to give it a few minutes. Two reasons: Anyone hit will bleed out and it is safer for the guys, and looks like it will be daylight in an hour or so and I would feel better about my guys going in there after it's light."

The waiting thing was something I was familiar with, being a hunter. So I sat down and tried to relax, but I noticed I never took my rifle down from a ready position while "relaxing." Seems that when hunting I have never had a deer shoot at me first.

I took out my magazine and saw that I must have fired about seven three-round bursts because I only had nine rounds in the mag. So I changed mags to feel comfortable that I had a full load if anything happened. Once we had been there for about twenty minutes or so I noticed that some of the usual night sounds started returning: frogs and night birds. I couldn't remember if they were there when we got out of the truck or not.

Once daylight started breaking and we could see, the Sergeant gave the order to move out into the woods to check the area but to keep low. Corporal Walters and I started out in a low profile and ready position. I glanced left and a line of about thirty or so troopers were moving into the trees. Again he told me to stay behind him and he made it clear that I was to point my rifle down because he didn't want a round in his backside if things were not as they appeared. He also said if we were to encounter any fire that I was to kneel down to his right and keep even with him so we had fields of fire that didn't overlap with friendlies or each other.

Our first discovery was the guy who we opened up on. He was clearly either Middle Eastern or Hispanic, but what made me think he was Middle Eastern were the baggy clothes he was wearing. I have seen that on countless photos coming back from the Iraq and Afghanistan conflicts. He was carrying an AK, and again he had a vest with multiple magazines in it but no armor. We continued to move straight ahead and the Corporal talked on the radio to someone farther up the line and said we were clear, and then we heard three other groups call in "Clear here, too."

After collecting their weapons, we all returned to the vehicles. I asked Walters if it was normal to pick up their weapons and he said "If we have time we do. We make sure they get destroyed so they won't be picked up and used by someone else."

Once back at the vehicles, I was listening to the troops talk about what they found and this time they found six dead enemy fighters. There were three black guys, two Hispanics with tats and one Middle Eastern. We added to the mix our Middle Easterner and now we had a ratio where of out of seven killed, two were Middle Eastern. Not promising. Looks like the Middle Eastern percentages were growing. I asked them how he could tell the difference, they said if you think about a native Indian and compare it to the person in front there was a difference in that the Middle Eastern held tight and close lines to the face, Indians didn't. That was the "tell."

I couldn't help but think about how our own countrymen (if they ever were part of our country) could turn on us this way. What was it that drove them to think that these scumbags from ISIS were a better solution than what we had right now in our country? Then it became clear that the people who used unrest and race as a wedge to make money had created a monster.

Or had they created what they set out to do?

I remembered the Soviet decree that they would bring down the US from within. No shots would be fired. They started by infiltrating the education system. Begin to swing the system to promote a liberal and Socialist education system that would teach that Socialism is good and that all are entitled to the same things. Then get control of the media— Once they had that it was all they would need. We would be taught that being an individual is bad but doing what everyone else does is good. Train them to see that what everyone else does is what they should do and they start to move in the Socialist lean. Our national education systems began pushing classroom teachings and text books that watered down the truth of what it took to build our country and what our true history of individual independence was. Slowly they would change the generational thinking to line up with a Socialist view. This would end the vision of what America could be as true individualists leaning on their own capabilities.

The biggest thing they wanted removed was the idealism it took to create our country and how the Declaration of Independence and our Bill of Rights were built based on the belief in God and a sound foundation of individual morals and ethics. I remember our current President saying that the Constitution was outdated. I disagree, the Constitution was created with a simple yet beautiful concept as its base, that people are responsible for their own decisions and ethics. However, if your base of ethics is not based on God's laws it is off base. But if our society is changed to be focused on a more socialistic view, then the Constitution would no longer work for the new Socialist population. But I believe the major core of our country is still based on individualism and the right to have the freedom to do what each person wants from a basis of freedom of religion and personal pursuit of freedoms.

The educational system and media have trained the people in our country to believe that they are downtrodden—that they were being abused because of their race. It was because the white man who had privilege hated the black and Hispanic. They would say this is supposed to be a land of opportunity and we should be open to anyone coming here, but if you were a minority that didn't apply. The truth is we were all minorities when we came here seeking religious freedom. All of that said by the left wingers was a smoke screen to overrun the red states. When the reality or true basis of truth was that the United States is the only free country where a man could take the initiative to build something and feel the pride that comes from the accomplishment, if they had the persistence and drive to do it. There is no other country on the planet with an open border policy and sadly the poor who flocked here were manipulated into believing they had an opportunity but were being played like a banjo. The leftist way of thinking was if we can get a lot of poor people into the country and convince them we were here to help them, then we can unseat the party that controls the conservative states forever. The conservative state believed in the constitution and that each man must provide for himself. For the leftists this was the only way to permanently deal with conservatives. It was all a game: Get the poor in here, tell them it is the land of opportunity and then vote for me because I made it all happen for you and I will give you everything you need. Sadly, by doing these things we were setting the stage for the perfect occupation by radical Islam.

Our Constitution and Bill of Rights represent a conservative ideal, given that freedom meant they could use our first amendment to say anything they wanted and to influence people to think that they were the victims. Our constitution allowed the opportunity for them to do exactly that. Then if a conservative voiced their view they would throw a Politically Incorrect flag on them to shut them up. Funny how the first amendment protected leftist teachings and not those of conservatives. They could also tell a low-information society controlled by a liberal media the things that were not true but were an emotional stimulus to get them fired up.

Once the education system was overhauled, next the media needed to be in control. If control of what is sent out is managed by the same group who sets the education criteria now, they would have the control they need to set the direction for the culture and the country. Somewhere in our country is a set of beating hearts that defines the strategy.

All of a sudden some things became crystal clear to me: With the events in Mississippi, what the media presented was a white cop who murdered a black unarmed man, when the reality was the black unarmed man was a robber and a bully and assaulted the cop, tried to take his gun before he could even get out of his car and then after walking away turned and charged the cop. The cop was outweighed by 150 pounds and it took six shots to stop the guy. But the story was never retracted with the facts. It was left to fester and breed discontent. The media became the breeding ground for the opportunity to use this group of people for sensationalism, which I guess sells copies but is a total lie.

Isn't it funny the progress of the poor and down trodden only works if they send checks to help the instigators who promote the cause? Funny isn't it, free enterprise which is our base is the very tool they would use to destroy everything our country was founded on.

CHAPTER 6:
SO NOW WHAT?

After I had my revelation I kept these things to myself because I knew these men were focused on two things: Doing their job and getting home alive. Deep philosophical discussions were not something they really cared about right now. But I could tell they were all disturbed by the events of the last couple of days and were trying hard to figure out what exactly was happening. After the debrief of the soldiers on what they had encountered and what we could do better next time, they all disbursed and went to find some chow, or MREs which aren't really chow but would keep you alive.

Once they all disbursed, I asked Sergeant Kyle if I could have a few minutes of his time. He said "I need ten minutes, then come find me."

I walked over to our transport and asked for a couple of fresh mags and asked the trooper there what he thought about what was going on. He said "This is messed up, man. We are fighting our own people. We are killing our own people. I am having trouble dealing with that." I said that is exactly what our enemy wants you to think about. These are not your people, these are people who hate the way of life that we call the American dream and they want to kill you and your family and they will stop at nothing to accomplish complete control of our country. You have got to see it that way or you will hesitate when it really gets ugly and they will not only kill you but they will hunt down your family and kill them too. I said "Soldier, do you know what the American dream is?"

He said "To be free and have the right to choose how you live."

"True, but think about this: Our country was founded on very different principles.

"The American Dream was actually an experiment. My grandfather fifteen generations back died in a London prison because he disagreed with the Church of England. His sons were put on a boat named the Anne in the year 1623 and were sent to the colonies as slaves or bond servants. They were treated as exiles to be sent to work in the Colonies. Once here, they had to work for ten years as slaves in order to achieve the status as free men. Once free men they got one acre of land and were then told "You are free to go and make a living for yourself, you are now on your own."

So they had to work for ten years just to earn the privilege of being on their own and try to scrape out a living for their family. One acre of land is just enough to raise the crops necessary to keep your family fed for the year, and that was a stretch. You needed to raise meat and crops to make it. So they learned how to trade crops for meat or raise meat and trade for crops. One bad year and you were done. But the people who came here believed a few common things: If you believed, God would provide what they needed and he always did. God would give you what you needed to make it if you just held on to the basic principles of truth and ethics and freedom and treated it as a precious thing.

"If we as a nation believe that there is no one entity we are accountable to such as God, then we remove the core of ethics and morals.This erodes the foundation our country was founded on. We are all accountable to God and so we must reconcile to him if we are to be complete as people." Then I looked at the young soldier who was looking at me like I was from another planet and said "But I digress. Let's get on with resupply of ammo and food so we survive this."

It takes time for people to absorb all of the stuff that has made us the country we were founded to be and the changes that have taken place to become the country we are today.

All of these young men were products of an education system that removed the founding principles from their teaching. It may take a long time to bring them to the point of realization and then to change. My greatest fear is that as humans we have a history of failure, and if that is true then we may be headed to the final conflict between good and evil.

So what is truth? I asked myself. I have come to realize that truth is what God says and everything else really doesn't matter. People have an opinion (which is all it is) but at the end of the day it changes nothing. So if you look at how our country was formed we were based on one thing, the truth of what God said and that was the most important thing in how we build and run a country.

Looking at our formation, the Founding Fathers said we will have a triune government, one that reflects the Godhead of Father, Son and Holy Spirit. We will form the Executive Branch, the Legislative Branch and the Judicial Branch. Each will have its own area to manage but all will be submissive to the triune character of God. Not to the Executive Branch, or Legislative or Judicial: only to God. Looks to me like the problem we have encountered in our country is that our leadership moved away from the truth of who God is, and the knowledge of His truth. Our current leadership has decided the timeless principles of the character of God are out of date and so our structure is failing. If you read the Constitution and the Bill of Rights, there is one assumed basic element and it is a core of ethics and morals that each person is individually responsible for. With freedom comes responsibility.

Then I remembered I was still trying to get to Galveston, wasn't sure how my wife was or even what I needed to do next. Reloaded and fed some more MREs, I was waiting like the rest to see what our next move would be. I also realized my life was going to be in the hands of the guys I was with for the foreseeable future.

I figured it had been about ten minutes, so I went looking for Sergeant Kyle. I found him with a map and another Sergeant leaning over the hood of a vehicle. I said "Sergeant Kyle, I have lived in Houston my whole life. Can I help you find something on the map?"

"Actually, maybe you can show us where you walked from." I pointed to the location on the north side and he said "Wow! That looks like a forced march distance."

"In cowboy boots and jeans it felt like it too."

"Now show us where you encountered problems on your route," he said, and I showed him the locations. Then I opened up and told him the whole story about the encounters and the shooting involved. He nodded and said "I figured it wasn't as easy as it sounded." I explained to them the areas of the city I figured would be hot zones with ISIS. I pointed to areas between 59 and I-45, areas west of I-45 and areas south and east of downtown. They looked at each other and nodded and said that sounded about right.

I said "As a consultant, I hate it when a client says that sounds like what we thought."

"Actually the verification is what we are looking for, so you did add value."

Then I pointed to Galveston and said it was where I needed to go. He showed me the area that had been compartmentalized and said "You won't make it right now. Even if you get close, the National Guard will stop you."

I also pointed to the area just south and east of Houston and said it would also mean I had to walk right through this area. My chance of survival on my own was getting smaller each passing minute. Kyle said "Well, here are your options. You can try to make it on your own or you can stay with us as a consultant. Your knowledge of Houston could be important to us."

"Well, looks like I'm now a consultant. I used to say that a consultant was just someone who was in between jobs, I guess that fits. You know another pair of boots to wear would be great." He laughed and said he'd get right on that.

Kyle pointed to the map and said "We have been ordered to hold this area of the east beltway." He was pointing at the area just north of I-45.

I told them "I figure the area around I-45 north of the belt is going to be the worst: It is the outside edge of the area south and east of downtown. Plus, there are a lot of shops in there and plenty of opportunity for looting. Cover will be a problem if you try to stay on the belt—it is elevated and wide open right there. However, there is a group of trees and some brush for cover right here..." I pointed to the southwest corner of the belt and I-45. "The top of the elevated ramp going from I-45 south to the east belt would be a great vantage point and maybe a sniper or two could be set up there. He would be out in the open but would have barrier walls and cars for cover. But it would be a long line of sight in all directions and we could hold off anyone trying to get up there."

I asked if he knew how widespread the EMP effect was and where power and comms were down. He outlined a basic circle that reached from Austin to nearly Galveston. I said "So Galveston wasn't knocked out."

"That's not what I said. I said this is the impacted area of the EMP, that took out the grid and power is off in most of the state of Texas."

I asked how long before power would get restored, and he said he was unsure because crews were taking fire trying to restore it. "With the EMP a lot of transformers are blown and it takes time to repair them. At some point we will probably have to be escorts so they can work on them without being shot at. But in this case darkness is our best friend. If they can't see us but we can see them it's to our advantage. We need to develop some intel on what the areas are like before we set up escort services." I asked if he had any status on Houston PD, he said only that they are totally engaged with riot control in several areas.

I asked "What about Galveston? I know most of those guys." He said most of their work is trying deal with casualties and restore a semblance of order. The law enforcement team in Galveston is one of the best trained groups in the country and I knew if it got thrown to them they would come through with high marks.

I said "So they are still trying to treat this as a police action and not a declaration of war?" He said "Yes for now. Most of the South Texas support is coming from county law enforcement in Harris, Montgomery, Galveston and a few others that cannot get much backup. Not to mention Galveston County just had a nuke detonate in Texas City and they are totally engaged in that. Some other state and local groups are trying to send help here but it takes time to move them with whatever support they will need. Plus, it will need to be from a county that did not feel the impact of the strike."

That statement made me wonder, so I asked Kyle "Did you have advanced notice this may be coming and that is how you got here so fast?"

"We were mobilized a few days ago and told that the chatter was off the charts and something big was coming. All of the National Guard in Texas was put on ready."

"Are we pulling back any combat troops to fight here in the US?"

"Not sure. That probably wouldn't happen until we complete our assessment."

"Anything being done to close and secure the border? Because it is an open highway for reinforcements and arms."

"A plan is being put together but I don't know how much progress has been made on that yet."

"As your new consultant, what can I do to help?"

"If I put you up on that overpass (and he pointed to the one I mentioned on the Beltway) with a sniper team, could you act as a forward observer and then give me feedback on how the areas around the freeway and the belt are doing?"

"Absolutely. When do we start?"

"I would like to move you guys in under the cover of darkness so you are not observed going in."

The rest of the day we continued to check out the areas around us and even left the belt to drive into some neighborhoods to see how things were going. Most of the neighborhoods outside the belt were stable, but there were lots of people outside their houses and talking in groups. We stopped to talk to as many as we could and most said they were ok for now but would need food and water soon. Luckily it was a cooler time of year and the heat wasn't a big problem. We also advised them to be on the lookout for roving groups who might be up to no good. As you might expect, since we are in Texas, there were plenty with firearms so we instructed them to form support groups and help each other until relief arrived, but to be sure and make themselves visible if military or police units came through. We also suggested they stay close to home and not go outside their local neighborhood.

We arrived back where the rest of the team was a little before sunset and they all seemed ready to roll. So we loaded up our two vehicles and started heading south on the belt. Once on the road the troops asked me what it was like in the neighborhoods we went through so I told them what we saw and what we told them to do. Just as it was dark we pulled up short of the overpass and set out three-man fire teams on each side of the road and a two-man team sent back behind us along the belt. Kyle handed me a pair of binoculars and told me very clearly "I want them back in one piece."

"Well, how about the vest? Do you want it back in one piece too?" He smiled. "That is Government issue. Those binocs are mine."

Then I started walking with a sniper and a spotter toward the overpass. Very slow and very low, that is what they told me. Not a problem, I told them. I was doing that anyway. We eased right into the lane turning north on I-45 and moved up on the top of the overpass working around a few stalled cars and I took the side facing to the north up I-45 and the other two set up looking south on I-45. On both sides we hugged up against the barrier walls or stalled cars for cover.

It was like in my old garage apartment before I got married: As soon as the light went out the roaches came out to explore. I could see through the binoculars that there was minor activity around the shops up and down the freeway. Then a bright flash and fire started in a car. Looked like a nice cocktail made from gasoline. You could hear glass breaking and groups of three to eight would go in the shops and leave with whatever they could carry. I am still confused that without electricity someone would think it was a good time to take a television, but I saw at least a dozen leave with TVs. The convenience stores were being cleaned out for what looked like snack food, beer, water and cigarettes. Houston Police rolled up and tried to disperse the crowds but they were heavily outnumbered and basically just took up defensive positions. They were in full riot gear with shields and batons but I could see some with ARs and shotguns as well.

By my rough count it looked like there were at least fifty people running around in the shop area and trying to break in. As they found locked doors, they started looking at windows, and soon the breaking of the windows started happening. Once the windows started breaking it was like a grouping call for turkeys in the fall, more people started showing up and going in the stores to take whatever they wanted. Now I figured the count had doubled to at least a hundred with more coming. I crawled back across to the guys on the other side and asked what they were seeing; they said not very much. I asked them how they wanted to report what I was seeing back or if we should wait until we left to tell the Sergeant what we'd seen. They said waiting is the best bet, but we could give him an update over the radio. As they were calling in the report I moved back over to my side.

Still watching the show going on I was amazed at how people had no regard for others' property — how they could see things as impersonal objects and just take them as though they were there for the taking. Because there was nothing the owner could do about it, all the stuff was free for the taking. I felt a disgust start to build toward these people and it wasn't even my stuff. This is not like what we see on Star Trek. Man is not evolving to a higher life form — in fact it looks like reverse evolution. Maybe we never found the missing link because it is in our future and we are evolving into monkeys.

Just then a Molotov cocktail flew from the crowd toward the police line. Police scrambled as it went off, throwing flaming fuel all over about a ten-yard area. Shotguns with bean bags and tear gas were launched into the crowd. Then the activity really went crazy, first rocks and then gun shots started coming from the crowd. I saw one police officer go down and then three others gathered around him with their riot shields and moved him to the back lines. It was escalating, now more gun fire from the crowd started, but it was not coming from the crowd in front it was coming from somewhere to the sides. This had been a setup for the police, draw them in, get an exchange going and then open fire on them. Much like what happened to us on the belt. The fire was intense and coming from both the right and the left of the police line.

I went back across the road and said to the other team "The police are being ambushed. Is there anything we can do?" They called it in on the radio and got a response that if we could locate the targets firing from the sides to take them out. "But do not engage if you are spotted. You need to get out of there and get back to us."

The sniper and spotter set up at the car I was at and I agreed to stay on the side they were on to watch our backs. It took a few minutes for the spotter to locate where the fire was coming from, and unlike the military team, the police had no heavy firepower to put on the attackers to discourage engagement. Then WHAM! — the first round went out.

I heard the spotter say "Tango down." About one minute later another wham, and another "Tango down." Then the fire from the right side started to ease up and the spotter switched to look at the left side. Wham, Tango down... then a quick wham, Tango down. After the second one on the left the fire from the sides stopped. So did the sniper, he just watched as the police tried to regroup and tend the wounded, they had three officers down.

I was watching my side looking south and saw some activity moving around on the freeway. Three guys moved out from the west side of the highway and started moving over to the ramp on the beltway turning south. That meant trouble for two reasons: They had communications with the others, and if they went up the ramp on that side they would have the high ground. I told the other two guys and I moved to a car for cover just behind us to cover the beltway ramp across from us. The other two did the same and we all got down in a prone position and went still. My weapon was pointed at the ramp and the safety was off. But instead of going above us they came over to the ramp we were on. That was a big mistake. I saw the three of them moving up very slowly and staying crouched to see if they could see anything. I could tell from the way they moved they were not sure if there was anyone up there but were told to check it out anyway. Just as they were about sixty yards on the down side of the ramp all three were cut down with what sounded almost like one shot, radios work for both sides. Kyle sent a fire team to cover our retreat.

Once we were sure they were down to stay we all got low and beat feet out of there to get back to the rest of the troops. I told the guys we should drag them down to the trees. As I went by the three I noticed that it was a little bit unusual to see all three were young black men, up until now there had been a mix of Hispanic and Middle Eastern with them. I grabbed their weapons as we went by, I handed one to the spotter and we dragged the bodies off the road and into the trees. We then kept going as fast as we could, now that we knew we had cover.

We met up with the rest of our platoon in about five minutes. It seemed like a lot longer because I kept looking over my shoulder the whole time. We met up with Sergeant Kyle at the vehicles and he said "OK, tell me what you saw."

We told him every detail and how the people were acting and how it looked like a trap for HPD. I told him about the numbers and how it looked like the same number we could see was waiting for the glass to start breaking and see if the police responded. "It seems funny that all three coming up behind us were young black guys. It seemed like most of the weapons and automatic stuff was saved for the police. I don't think they know we're here yet. It is also something that the three only had pistols and a shotgun. Not as heavily armed as the guys firing on the police. So I would say they have limited resources right now but they are obviously building in troop strength and I am sure the weaponry will start showing up too. Looks like they think in these areas the police are their biggest threat. Sad… They might as well have sent knife fighters to a gunfight as sent those guys up the ramp. It also tells me they were not sure where the shots came from but figured they had better send someone up to check it out. By dragging the bodies off into the brush they will probably figure they bailed out and went somewhere else. It may buy us some time to do some more recon."

Kyle looked at me and said "Are you sure you were not in the military?"

"Positive. I got drafted for Vietnam but failed the physical because of a sports injury. That was about the best thing high school did for me. But I did play a lot of video games."

Then he turned to his drivers and said "I want those vehicles off in the woods on the south side of the belt right there," and pointed to a grove of trees. "Cover them with branches but make sure we have a field of fire for the 60 if we need it. Corporal, make sure our fire teams are hidden and all have radios. I want to pick and choose who shoots and at what, and do it NOW!"

CHAPTER 7:
OK, THIS IS CRAZY

We all got deep in cover and the fire teams were in position with one three-man team to our left and one to the right, the sniper and the spotter went to look for a spot to provide cover while the two-man team went behind us. I sat with the Corporal and the Sergeant watching directly in front. These guys were good at camouflage—you couldn't see the trucks, and even the tire tracks going off the road were smoothed over. With daylight coming, it was probably best to hang tight and not get out there to make ourselves visible just yet. It is always best to know what you are up against and not pull a George Custer and just charge in.

While with these two men I started thinking about how America had some of the finest warriors in the world and how politics had misused them yet they still fought and fought hard and smart. I could see in their eyes that there was something different about this time, now they had a lot of personal skin in the game. Before they were fighting for each other, this time they were fighting for each other and their families, their futures and their buddy next to them and their buddy's family and future. Kyle got a call on his radio and moved off to take it while the Corporal and I sat there mostly silent. When Kyle returned he said "We are now getting reports of public executions by ISIS in the neighborhoods where they are setting up shop."

I said "Well, that is one way to build an army, but it didn't work out too well for Hussein. The problem is: How do we root them out and kill them without blowing up neighborhoods? They will use human shields like they do everywhere else. Do we have that kind of surveillance and targeting intel?"

Kyle said "Not just yet. We are redirecting most of our satellites over our soil now to get a better picture of what is going on. We have drones in the air as well and they are starting to set search patterns and grids. So far we don't have much intel from the ground in those areas, seems most of the people being executed were former military and were seen as threats right away. We should be getting some SEAL teams as well as other dark ops in here over the next few days to get in there and give us a view from the ground."

I said "Once the physical threats are removed they will move to the philosophical threats like any religion not Muslim."

I asked the Sergeant if he knew of any civilian militias being formed. He said he didn't know but he figured it would be inevitable. I said "Especially here in Texas. We don't like this kind of stuff. Has any thought been given to a coordinated effort with the military once the militias start forming? I mean after all you used warlords in the Middle East, why not cowboys in Texas? We have better firepower and with a little help from the US Army we could secure neighborhoods in a lot of areas."

"Not that I've heard of, but it could become a factor soon. If power stays out and law enforcement is not returned within the next few days it could get really hairy around here."

"My bet is ISIS will do everything it can to keep the power down and to keep chaos building; this is how they establish themselves as the local authority. My guess is they will have strong presence around grid locations to make sure it doesn't come back on till they are ready for it too. I would also bet they will wait until they can take the credit for it when it does come back on. Then they control the local areas and once they have local authority they begin the purge of the infidels."

America had never seen the type of anti-Christian and anti-freedom persecution that could be coming our way. It made me wonder about the church in America and if it truly had to face persecution if it would stand or if it would fall. Would they fight or convert to Islam? What scared me the most was I didn't know. I had to believe that history has shown that the more Christianity is persecuted the stronger it becomes, but America is not the Christian nation it once was. While we call ourselves Christians we do not actually live it, we have become a country that is more about self-satisfaction than self-sacrifice, we have replaced our core values with the ideal of "if it doesn't impact me I don't care."

Now we could be faced with something much more sinister than when we fought for our independence, this time fighting for everything we currently hold dear. I could see the potential of the traditional Christian church going away. Everything we were built to be as a nation could fall to Sharia law. America the Late.

I asked the Sergeant if he had heard anything from Galveston, he said he hadn't but would ask for me. I thanked him and told him about where I lived and about the view of the bay and how the sunrise and sunset both were awesome from our deck. I told him "When all this is over, you need to sit on the deck with me and have a glass of red wine and watch the seabirds. I said I may be able to get the smoker going if we have electricity by then."

He laughed and said "I bet we have it back on and I will take you up on that offer."

I also told him I was really worried about my wife. Our house faces the north and we are only about three or four miles as the crow flies from Texas City. I told him about the lights from the refineries and how it looked like Christmas all year round, but when I looked at him he had grown dark. I said "What is the matter?"

"The only report I have from there is that the fallout and chemical leaks really hit that area hard. I hope she is OK." He turned back to look at the road in front of us. That pretty well put a damper on my state of mind. I turned and looked at the road as well.

A brief break in on the radio said a small group of about five were walking down the beltway headed north. They came from I-45 and it looked like a patrol. The Sergeant said "Let them pass but put a tail on them to see where they go. Stay in cover. We don't need any shooting to give away our position."

I asked the Sergeant "Do you have any silenced weapons?"

"No, that's for Special Ops, typically."

I asked if he thought they could be captured and he said "Probably, but what would we do with them after we have them? I don't have enough men to watch prisoners."

"Well, you wanted intel. Is there a better way than getting it from the horse's mouth?"

"You may have a point. Let's see how far down the road they go." Then he told two other troopers "Go with the one following them. If they get far enough away where the shots would be hard to figure out a direction then take them. We only need one or two alive. Kill the others, and the survivors may be in a talking mood. Once you take them pull them off in the woods to hide them and radio me. I want to interrogate them."

The troopers set out following along the tree line and in stealth mode. These guys were good. I watched them go out of sight over the rise about a mile and a half back, and then I heard several shots. I counted about five and then silence. Almost immediately Kyle got a radio message saying two prisoners were secured and the other three were KIA. I had to think that these guys were really good because they waited until the group crossed over the rise on the belt so the sound would be muffled and direction was nearly impossible to figure out. Kyle told his troops to stay on their station and keep low, not to engage unless engaged and to call him if they see anything. Kyle and I set out down the side of the road to get to their location as fast as we could.

After we walked over the hump which was Highway 3 to Galveston a trooper stepped out of the tree line and waved. We walked over to him and he said "They are in the woods about ten yards off the road," and crouched and stayed there on watch while we made our way in. We found the other trooper and two guys bound in tie wrap handcuffs on his hands and feet with a piece of tape over their mouths. I asked Kyle if all his guys carried tie wraps and tape, and he said "Absolutely. Duct tape is a handy man's best friend. I once heard that if the women don't find you handsome they need to find you handy." One of our captives was Hispanic and one was Middle Eastern: ISIS, we figured.

We talked to the ISIS guy first. Kyle said to cover him, so I held my .40 cal up to his head and Kyle took the tape off after saying "If you yell out he will shoot you." As soon as the tape came off he went crazy yelling, so I shot him. Kyle looked at me and said "OK, next."

He removed the tape from the other guy and I held the gun to his head. Kyle said "Did you see what just happened?" He nodded, so Kyle said I am only going to ask you these questions once so be as honest and accurate as you can be, or he will shoot you too." He nodded and said OK.

Kyle asked "Who is telling you what to do?" He said some Middle Eastern guys, and he only knew one named Muhammad. "Are you kidding me? His name is Muhammad?" "Yes, that is what they call him."

"How many Middle Eastern guys are there now?" "Four."

"How many others do you have with you who is doing the fighting?" "About 50 so far."

"What kind of weapons are they carrying?" "Mostly AKs but there are some ARs, some grenades. A couple of RPGs."

Kyle asked him how long the cartels have been supporting the smuggling of arms and Middle Eastern guys into the US. He said about a year or so. Kyle asked him if he had any idea how many came across the border: He said no. Kyle asked him where he came from and what was happening in the neighborhood he just came from. He said we are just across I-45 on the south side of the belt and right now it is a little crazy because everyone is mostly just looking for stuff to steal before the power comes back up.

Kyle picked up his radio and walked away a little distance. He radioed for a pickup of the prisoner and was told that a truck was on its way. When Kyle walked back he asked the prisoner if he could tell us what the next plan of action was. He said "The ISIS guys are trying to build up supporters and they are giving everyone weapons. They are also coaching them on what to do and how and when to attack."

Kyle asked him are there any who are refusing, the guy said yes but they shot them execution style and everyone cooperated after that. Kyle then asked him where is the center of operations and where are they storing the weapons. The guy said they had taken over a building just south on I-45 one street back from the freeway and they had the weapons in the building so they could hand them out. There was a line of people waiting to get guns when he was sent out on patrol. Kyle asked if he could find that place on a map, and the guy said "I don't know. Maybe."

Kyle pulled out the map and the guy looked at it for a long time and said "I think it is about here." Kyle said "OK, what's your name?" He said it was Emilio. Kyle asked if he was from the US or from another country. "I am from Venezuela."

Kyle stood up and walked over to one of his men and said "Soldier, get some tape back on that guy and make sure he doesn't go anywhere and that he stays quiet. Before you tape him see if he wants a drink of water." Then Kyle walked out of the woods and to the soldier watching the highway. He said "You stay here until transport arrives for the prisoner, then both of you double time it back to us as soon as you can. Tell the pickup not to drive you to us; we don't want anyone seeing we are there."

The soldier said "Yes sir," and Kyle and I started walking back to the cover spot. As always, we walked on the side of the road and watched a full 360° around us. He said "You know, usually the 'shoot him' thing is a bluff to get them to talk." I said I had heard that didn't work on the radicals. He said it sure worked on the other guy.

Once back to the camp we filled in Corporal Walters on what the prisoner had to say. He said "Can you show me on the map where he said the building was?" We pointed to the spot. He said "Sergeant, do you want me to send a recon?"

Kyle looked at him and said "That is really dangerous, but do you think from the overpass you were on if you were watching that area we might have a different view of what we are looking at? Walters said "Possibly. If we send our spotter and the sniper to have a look-see they are trained observers." I said "I can go too. After all, I am now a consultant, and we are trained observers, and two or three pairs of eyes are better than one." Kyle said "OK, let's do it, but if you guys get in trouble we will have to roll out of our location to help you. So try not to get killed tonight, we need to stay here to see what is happening in this area." I asked Kyle if he had a pair of boots I could use and he said he would get right on that.

We collected our gear and again I was told I better bring the binoculars back in one piece and we set out. I asked if I could have a grenade or two. They asked me if I had ever used one before. I said no and they just laughed and handed me the extra magazines. I asked the soldier if he had any .40 cal ammo and he said actually he did. He handed me a box of .40s, and I grinned and dropped them in my vest. This time I felt better about carrying extra ammo because now I knew there were at least fifty bad guys and more being recruited each minute. I loaded my Sig clip to capacity and checked my AR mags to make sure I was full as I walked.

We made it up the overpass without anything happening, and this time we crawled along the barrier until we had a good view on the downhill slope of the area we wanted to look at. Luckily, there were stalled cars and we found a nice Ford F-250 to crawl under. The spotter and I crawled up against the wall to look over the area and the sniper got in the bed of the truck looking back at the overpass to watch our backs.

We started seeing activity in the general area almost as soon as we set up. The spotter started making calculations on the location of the building and radioed them back to Kyle to have an exact position. Ten minutes later there was a tremendous explosion and the building exploded from within. I said "Holy smoke, man, did you know that was coming?"

He said "I figured that would happen. We have National Guard air support up and flying high altitude standby for about three hours now."

"Next time, give a guy some warning! I was nearly over the wall when that thing went off." He said "Sorry."

I asked "Can you check my pants? I need to know if they are wet anywhere, so I don't chafe." He chuckled and said "Come on, we need to go now."

We eased back down the overpass and got back to the camp without any issues. Once there, Kyle said "Good work, you guys. Did you confirm the strike?" The spotter said "Yes sir, clean hit."

Kyle said "OK, you guys, settle in, because it will be daylight soon and we will need to hunker down for a while." I found a nice soft tree to lean up against and settled in for a little nap.

I woke up when the sun was overhead at about the 11:00 position and was shining directly on me, and it was getting warm. I realized I had been trying to get to Galveston for four days, not counting the present day. I managed to stand up with a lot of creaking and popping and found a few guys sitting around heating up their MREs.

I noticed there was no fire but they looked like they were eating warm stew. I said "How did you guys heat that?" They said "Look at the package. There are heating elements in it. All you do is add water and you have stew."

Awesome! Maybe MREs aren't so bad! I fixed one, and sure enough, it did get warm—but it still didn't taste that great. However, considering my other options, it would do just fine. I noticed my pants were fitting a lot better; I must have lost ten or fifteen pounds in the last three days. Man, this was a crash diet like no one has seen before. Even my boots were more comfortable, so I decided to take them off. Big mistake: Smelled like road kill. So I left them off only long enough for my socks to dry some and then I put them back on.

Kyle walked in to grab something to eat and I asked him if we had any activity on the road this morning. He said nothing really to speak of, only a patrol or two. It looked like they were looking for their buds more than they were looking for us, so we didn't interfere. He said

"Everyone get some rest. Tonight we are moving, and we are going into the area we hit yesterday, so it might get crazy."

I looked around at the other guys and they went silent and looked at each other. I knew that meant we could get into some deep stuff tonight. The second time you go into an area they will be more prepared for you.

CHAPTER 8:
WHO OWNS THE NIGHT?

That afternoon, the troops sat down to clean their weapons and get prepared for the night. The watch posts had gone down to a rotational basis with just one guy at a time on watch in each location. I watched as each one took apart their ARs and cleaned everything, and I did the same. I have never taken an AR down to that level before so it was an educational experience to watch. It also made me feel better about the state of my weapon before combat.

I could feel the jitters starting and watched how these guys handled it: They were very matter of fact and businesslike in their preparation. Each moving part was inspected, light oil was applied, every bullet was checked before going in the magazine. All the belts and gear were checked and rechecked. Straps were tightened with nothing but pure focus.

Just before dark, everyone grabbed another quick bite to eat and slugged down some water. Kyle walked up and said "OK, listen up: We are going into the area we observed yesterday to check on the building air cover hit last night. I expect resistance, and from what we know there could be from fifty to a hundred armed resistors there waiting for us. They know the area so they will have the cover already set up. We will go low and slow and we will check every corner, every roof top, and every alley and never go off point. Keep your heads on a swivel and watch the roofs. We will break into three-man fire teams with no group ever being more than a block away from the other. We will move directly to the building from all four sides, front, sides and rear. Check it out with a three man team while the others cover, do a damage assessment and then get out of there. Are there any questions?" No one had any.

He said "OK saddle up. This time we ride. Porter, you have the 50 cal. Go check it out and make sure it is ready to rock. We will have an Apache in orbit waiting in case it gets too hairy. But I am hoping we get in and get out without any problems."

We removed all the tree branches on the vehicles for cover and loaded up. I looked at our nice comfortable little hiding spot and realized we wouldn't be back here. We were going in harm's way. Now I really had the jitters—this was the first time I had had time to think about it and get ready and I was more nervous than ever before.

The first vehicle rolled out on the belt and we followed at about a hundred feet. We started rolling at dusk and were on the overpass in four minutes. We weaved between stalled vehicles and exited the first exit on I-45 south. We hung an immediate right and started toward the building. We stopped two blocks from it and everyone dispersed out of the vehicles and formed the fire teams. Man these guys were good: They checked everything and their weapons were always up in front of their eyes and wherever they looked the rifle went with them. One team went straight, one went right and one left. We followed to go to the front of the building. Each team had one watch our 6 to make sure there were no surprises. I was in a team with Corporal Walters and a young trooper named Higgins. Corporal Walters took the group that went to the back of the building.

We all stopped at the first corner and watched as the rear unit and the three side units went to their positions: So far so good. We got three clicks on the radio which meant that everyone was in position. They pointed weapons away from the building to cover us and we went in what used to be the front of the place: mostly debris now. We stepped in and started making our way deeper inside.

Kyle told the trooper to find cover and cover the front in case we need an exit. As Kyle and I went inside we saw some bodies in the building. We estimated four at least, but they were splattered all over everything. It was hard to tell how many. A missile is pure devastation on the inside of a building.

We went through into the next set of rooms and found what must have been the weapons stash. Lots of broken cement and busted up rifles, mostly weird stuff but also a few AKs—even a few ARs were in there. It didn't look like very many of them would be of any use to anyone now.

Then we heard fire from the side of the building facing south. We heard radio transmissions saying they were engaged with a half dozen or more: assistance needed. We started to move back to the front of the building and then fire came from the back as well. The radio said we have Tangos in back too, at least four. Just then the other side lit up too, now we had bad guys on every side but the front. Kyle asked the trooper out front if he saw anything—"Nothing, sir."

We moved back up front and as we did we came under fire from the building next door. It looked like there were three in there blocking our exit. We at least had cover but the guys outside were in trouble.

Over the radio came "man down!" from the group in the rear of the building, so I told Kyle I was going to try and work my way through the building to see if there was a back door I could let them in by. I started making my way—and the going was hard, lots of cement to climb over—but I reached the back and found a door. I stepped to the side and tried to open it but there was debris blocking it. So I started moving the debris and finally had a space where I could get the door opened.

I eased it open and looked for our guys; just as I did, bullets hit the wall about a foot from my head. I ducked back in and called out to the team in back, asked if they could make it to the door. They said they could, but they would need cover. I said "OK, on my *Go* I will give cover and you haul it over here. *GO!*"

I swung around and started putting three-round bursts into the building next door at the places I figured they might be. Here came one, then another and now we had two of us putting down cover fire: Walters made it in safely.

Walters said "Look for windows to shoot from. There has to be something in this wreck." We eased back to check out the area when an RPG hit the door we'd been standing at. The concussion knocked me and Walters down, but we recovered quickly. My ears were ringing to beat the band. Walters said "Take cover! They may try to come in."

I found a chunk of floor that had fallen in and got behind it with my rifle on the door. The other soldiers moved into the next room to see if they could find a window. Walters set up behind a pillar and also covered the door.

We heard the guys on the sides of the building were still in it, but so far no one had tried to come in the back. Then a grenade rolled in and we both hit the ground and covered our ears: *Wham!*

The concussion was rough and shrapnel ricocheted all of over the room. But we were OK. Then two guys came in the door and were nailed immediately. After that no one else tried to come in.

The other guys found a window and said they could cover the door and for us to move to the front of the building. We moved, got to the front and found Kyle and the other trooper still exchanging fire with the building across from us.

I said "Now might be a good time to call in air support."

"I already did."

About that time the building across from us blew from the inside out. Kyle shouted orders for everyone to regroup in front and get to the vehicles. They came from both sides, plus the two who were with us covering the windows, formed fire teams, and started moving back to the vehicles. One team was in front, a team was watching our 6, and the rest of us were in the middle.

One of the guys coming from the side was hit. It looked like a shoulder hit, so I helped carry him along with another trooper and we started moving the two blocks to our vehicles. We were in the same block and more fire opened up from the building ahead, blocking our route to the vehicles.

Porter on the M60 was keeping fire on the building between us and the vehicles. Kyle called in for air support and said "Danger close, danger close: The building to our northeast has hostiles in it. Take them out."

He turned to us and said "Everyone get down. Find some cover if you can. This could get ugly."

Porter backed up with the vehicle and we retreated as far as we could to find cover. Within thirty seconds a missile hit the building ahead and then some 20 mm cannon fire pasted the whole front of the building.

Kyle radioed back: "Thanks: We are on the move."

Porter said "Stay where you are. We are coming around the block closer to you." Then he pulled up right in front of us, and we hauled it to the vehicles. I helped get the wounded trooper in the transport and we rolled out of there. Porter covered our exit with the 60.

We made it back out onto I-45 and headed for the ramp to the belt back the way we came. The wounded soldier was being attended by two other soldiers and they reported they needed to get Medevac for him. Walters was on the radio calling for a chopper and gave them the location where we would be on the beltway. We pulled up at the spot we had been at earlier and set a defensive perimeter around our location and made sure there was an area for the chopper to land. In about 15 minutes a chopper flew in and they transferred him to the bird and then they were gone. Once the chopper left it seemed to get really quiet, everyone watched the bird leave and stayed on their post with distant expressions.

Kyle had everyone move back into the positions we'd had earlier and said "You know where to go: Get there and stay frosty."

Again I sat with Kyle and Walters. I asked what the next move was. They said "For now we hold this area. We will take an occasional patrol to see what is happening but we stay here for now."

We sat there for a long three or four minutes and then Kyle said "Let's debrief on what just happened." I told him what had happened once I'd gone inside to find the back door and what I had seen in the arms stash. I told him about the back door, the guys coming in the back door, the RPG, the grenade, and the two we shot coming in the door.

Walters told him about the rear of the building and that they were in position in the building behind it waiting. He said the fire was coordinated from the bad guys, once the rear opened up all sides did. I asked Kyle "Did you notice that they didn't come in through the front? Instead, they were waiting to cut off our retreat to the vehicles. It seems strange that they didn't open up on us as soon as we pulled up."

"Think about it. If they have teams set for every side they needed to wait until we dispersed and they had smaller groups to engage with. Then if the smaller groups didn't finish us they had our retreat to the vehicles covered. It was a really good ambush strategy. I saw this same tactic when I was in Iraq. The house to house stuff is what they are good at. Their biggest miscalculation was they figured we were still treating this like a law enforcement issue and we wouldn't have air cover. They won't make that mistake again."

I started thinking, *War has come to the United States, and whether we like it or not, we are in a fight for our survival.* I think it was just starting to settle in with me, because up until this point I was still trying to get a handle on what was happening and who the enemy was. I looked at Kyle and said "Sergeant, I know I am a new consultant for you, but I need to take a leave of absence. I have got to try and make it to Galveston. This is going to get real ugly and I can't do this without knowing what is happening at home."

"I figured that was coming." He pulled out the map. "What is your strategy to get there?"

I showed him how there are trees and brush all along the west side of I-45 but once I got to NASA Road 1 and on to Dickenson I would be exposed. So I pointed to Highway 3. "It runs parallel to I-45 and it has less density of stores and looting targets. I can move after dark and stay to the brush as much as possible. All along the highway here to here is the border for Ellington Air field that may give me cover. Plus if I had some wire cutters I could get inside the high fence and it would be a lot harder for outsiders to get to me. Wire cutters would also make cross country travel through the fields a lot easier too. I'll move back to I-45 once I reach El Dorado Blvd—then I know I'll have cover in the fields and will only have a couple of exposure points at bridges where I have to cross water. At those I will have to walk out in the open."

"You do know you will be by yourself the entire way? I can't send anyone with you."

"I know, but I have to do this. If you can spare a radio, I would report back what I am seeing as I go, sort of like a long-distance recon mission." He said that could be done.

We went to the back of the transport. He looked in a tool box and handed me a pair of wire cutters. Then he handed me a radio and said

"Use this frequency." He looked at me from head to toe and said also "You may need a few more mags. Listen, keep the binocs but they better come back in one piece."

"Where have I heard that before? So does that mean I can keep the rifle?"

"It's government issue. You can bring it back to me later."

"Do you have a pair of size 12 boots I could use?"

"I will get right on that."

"It's a deal," I said, and slugged down two bottles of water, putting a couple more in my vest along with two MREs. I said "I am not really sure what to say at this point. You guys are heroes, and it has been an honor fighting with you. Goodbye, and I will see you later."

As I started away, I turned to Kyle and said "What if I find others who are willing to fight? Could you use them?"

"Call me, we can discuss it."

"If I run into other units between here and there, can I drop your name?"

"Sure." He got on the radio and told his team I was pulling out and heading back toward Highway 3 "So don't punch any holes in him."

With that I started walking again.

CHAPTER 9:
THERE AND BACK AGAIN

Highway 3 used to be the old Galveston highway years ago, but once I-45 was built, it has become just an alternate route when I-45 is too clogged up. There are a lot of subdivisions around there, most of them populated by NASA employees or contractors working for NASA or at the airport. I figured that since I left the camp at about midnight I might have a good four or five hours to make some headway and look for a good place to get cover before daylight. At this hour it was pretty quiet. I saw an occasional person walking in singles or pairs, and they didn't appear to be armed.

I didn't need to cut the fence, and I found pretty good cover in fields on the west side of Highway 3. There were still lots of bushes and some small trees for cover so that made moving fairly efficient. I made it to El Dorado and turned right. This area made me real nervous.

I knew there were apartments on the left just before the freeway so I tried to stay behind buildings on the right and move low and slow to get through them. I made it to the I-45 overpass and realized it had taken longer than I figured and I needed to get across the overpass and hide in the brush in the fields on the west side. I got low and went over

I-45 on the overpass. I moved down the feeder road about two hundred yards and cut the top wire on a fence and went into the field to find some trees for cover. I moved about a hundred yards back from the freeway close to highway 646 and settled in a grove of live oaks. I sat down and started trying to cool off from the walk. From here I could see parts of the freeway and the field behind me was open. This area felt pretty safe and I had a good field of fire.

I had grown used to the quiet, and when I heard a vehicle on the freeway, I took notice. I looked through the binocs and saw two pickup trucks moving slowly down the freeway. Uh oh: There were guys in back with guns. I couldn't tell if they were friendly or not so I just watched them roll through.

About five minutes later I heard an exchange of gunfire from about a mile down the road. I couldn't tell what was going on, so I decided to move out closer to the road to see if I could tell with the binocs what was happening. I saw a blockade that had been set up about a mile away and there was both police and National Guard there, exchanging fire with the trucks. Then one of the trucks driving into the barricade blew up: Looked like a car bomb.

They had let them get too close. I guess the police were still treating this as a typical disaster event and not using wartime protocols. It looked like several officers and a couple NG guys were down. The second truck threw it in reverse and started trying to back out of there as fast as possible.

Fire opened up from the remainder of the blockade troops, but the truck made a turn and was headed back down the freeway toward me. It was almost daylight so it would be hard to see me in the early morning against a stalled vehicle. I could see about three guys were in this vehicle. Without even thinking I moved out to a stalled car in front of me and set up with a rest.

Once the truck was within eighty yards of me I opened up on the driver. I could tell he took one in the head. The truck swerved and then rolled and stopped about fifty yards from me. The other two guys went flying out onto the freeway. One of them tried to get up so I dropped him. The other one seemed to be too hurt to get up so I saved the rounds.

I looked at the blockade, and a chase vehicle was starting my way. I quickly raised my rifle over my head and stood still. They pulled up and started yelling for me to drop my weapon. I said "I am a friendly! I just left the 36th to do some recon south. You can check with Sergeant Kyle on this frequency." I handed the first officer my radio.

Two NG team members checked the three guys that were down. One walked over to me with his weapon raised and said "Put down your weapon." I complied.

The Dickenson police officer who I recognized as a guy who stopped me for speeding last December looked me up and down and said "Why are you wearing cowboy boots?"

"That is a long story. Do you mind if I put my hands down? I have a sidearm too—do you want it as well? I do have a permit to carry it."

He asked where it was. Under my vest, I said. Show it to me, he said. I lifted my shirt and he asked for some ID, so I handed him my CHL and my driver's license. "You can keep it," he said. "Do you know any of these guys?"

"No, but I have come to know their types over the last few days."

"What do you mean by that?"

"Well, I have been in a few firefights with Sergeant Kyle's National Guard unit around the beltway and I-45 and have been working as a consultant for his team because I know Houston pretty well. But I live in Galveston so once they got settled in the area they are holding I set out for Galveston."

"You mean you walked here?"

"Well… technically, I have walked from the Woodlands to here. "

"Holy smoke, how far is that?"

"Not sure, but I know from my house on Tiki to my office is about 76 miles."

The two National Guard soldiers checked the three casualties by the overturned vehicle and collected their weapons. Again, it was a Middle Eastern guy behind the wheel and two young black men in the back. Then the officer got on his radio and talked to the team behind him. The NG team asked if he could bring me back to talk with them. He said "Come with me. The guys at the blockade want to talk to you."

"Does that mean I can ride?"

"Yep. Get in."

I climbed in the back seat next to another NG guy. I turned to him and said "Have you ever ridden in the back seat of a squad car before?"

He grinned and said "Once."

"Well, this is my first time. It smells like puke back here." The two in front laughed.

We pulled up at the blockade and the two in front had to let us out since there were no door handles in the back seat. The officer said to follow him and we walked over to where a Medevac team was working on the downed police and NG team members. The officer, who according to the name on his shirt was Corporal Hayes, said "Captain, this is the guy we found. His name according to his ID is Terrell." The officer handed me back my IDs and said "I will leave your weapon over here." Then Hayes walked over to check on the condition of the wounded.

It was daylight now and I could see the name on the captain's shirt said Morgan, I said "Really? You are Captain Morgan?" He smiled and said yep. I said "It's nice to meet you, sir." and I reached out my hand to shake.

He shook my hand and said "I got a radio message from Kyle last night that said you might be headed this way. Kyle said you are pretty good in a fight."

"Well I don't know how good I am, but I do know how to shoot and when I'm scared I can be pretty accurate." I asked him which group he was with and he said he was with the National Guard in Texas City.

Morgan asked me what I had seen on Highway 3. I told him when I went through there it seemed pretty quiet but I stayed in cover most of the way and tried to avoid any contact. I said "There may be a few fences to repair back along my route. Ellington was real dark and most of the neighborhoods along there were still. An occasional walker, but for the most part all seemed quiet."

Morgan asked me if I knew the status of Galveston. "Well," I said, "Only what I got from Kyle. He said it had been compartmentalized and no one goes in or out."

"That's right. We are set up here to turn around anyone trying to go in."

"Do you have any damage or casualty reports coming out of the Galveston area yet?"

"A few, and they are all really bad. Looks like the biggest problem wasn't the nuke; the biggest problem was the chemical releases. The refineries took the nuke: Marathon, Sterling and Valero took it the hardest. Looks like from the air it was a car bomb nuke and they drove in between two refineries to pop it. We think the chemicals will dissipate in a day or so, and we can start sending some hazmat crews in to check."

"Any way I can go with? I can help with the armed escort."

"Maybe. I will check for you."

I asked Morgan if he'd had any other vehicles try to approach them beside these two. "Just one," he said, "and we turned them around."

"Were they Hispanic, Black or Middle Eastern?"

"They were Hispanic and they had family in Texas City and drove down from San Antonio to check on them. They had valid Texas IDs from San Antonio and we had no reason to hold them so we sent them back."

"Maybe they were probes, checking your defenses. Did you search their vehicle?"

"No, we didn't have a reason to."

"They most likely went back and told the others what was here, and they sent the trucks. There is very little vehicle traffic in the city right now. They had to bring them in from outside the range of the EMP.

"They have a solid plan and have sleeper cells standing by all over the country waiting for the go-ahead. These guys are probably rolling in from West and deep South Texas to fight. Most likely they had their vehicles in underground garages to protect them from the EMP. These guys are getting some serious firepower too. We blasted a weapons cache in Houston just inside the belt that could have armed a hundred fighters. We were fired on by automatic weapons, RPGs, and hand grenades. Did Kyle tell you about the guy we captured?"

"Yes. We're waiting for a report on the intel that was gathered at our base of operations."

"Captain, any other questions I can answer, or anything I can do for you?"

"Not at this time."

"OK if I stay with you a while till the chems dissipate and I can go on toward Tiki. I would be happy to work the barricade if I could have my weapon back."

"Considering I just lost two soldiers and the police lost three, you're welcome on the line."

"Do you have a pair of boots in size 12?"

"I will get right on that. Kyle told me to tell you he wants those binocs back in one piece."

"You guys are all alike," I complained, smiling. He smiled back and walked to his vehicle.

I picked up my weapon, checked the mag and walked to the line. There was a lot of concern on the faces of the two policemen and the five soldiers who were still healthy. I walked in beside the two policemen and said "Hey guys, you doing OK?"

"OK… considering."

"Understood. Do you know what's happening in Houston and the big cities up and down the Eastern Seaboard?"

"Not entirely."

I explained about the nukes, the EMPs and how the sleeper cells were being rallied. I told them about the types of fighters we had run into and that ISIS was behind all of it. They stood there in silence listening. Once I had finished talking Corporal Hayes, the trooper who had stopped me on my speeding adventure, asked if I thought we were at war. I said "My bet is Yes. The trick is if our government will accept that and do something about it now before ISIS gets a stronghold in our major cities. By the way, I know I said thank you when you stopped me on I-45 that day for speeding and didn't write me up but just to make doubly sure: Thank you."

He smiled and said "So if this gets ugly, you owe me one?"

"That's a fact: I got your back."

"Well, I was thinking that I might have doubts about someone I wrote a ticket to but if you cover me I will write you another warning next time."

"Oh, well, alrighty then! Next time I will insist that you write me a warning." We both laughed.

I pulled up the binocs and started a scan of the road and the areas around us to check things out. Nothing was happening. All seemed quiet. About an hour later, I thought I saw movement down the road. I picked up the binocs and saw two guys moving from vehicle to vehicle for cover. I said "Morgan, we have movement on the road."

He came over and asked where. I said "I just saw two guys moving back and forth in between the cars about three hundred yards from us."

"Do you see any vehicles?"

"Not yet. For just a second I thought it looked like they may be carrying an RPG." He issued the order down the line to spread out, stay behind cover and to watch for incoming RPGs.

"That will make pucker marks in some breeches."

"Mine too, since I had just been on the receiving end of one yesterday. Have you got a sniper or anyone with long range optics?" He said no.

"What if we have two guys move up the side of the road a hundred yards from us toward them and set up to ambush them when they move within range for the RPG?"

"Great idea, Terrell. You go and take another soldier with you... Riley! Get over here! Go with Terrell, here."

We eased out of the blockade and moved just inside the fence line back up the freeway. We set up 100 yards from the blockade in the woods looking at a stalled vehicle we figured would be the closest they could get and still have some accuracy with the RPG. Then we waited.

It was full daylight but we were betting on the fact they would be focused on the barricade and we might have an element of surprise. It didn't take very long, maybe seven or eight minutes, and here they came. Two guys snuck up to the car thinking they were really going to give the blockade a surprise. Just as they settled down and checked the RPG I told Riley "I have the one on the left. You take the one on the right. On my mark…"

I cut down the one on the left and he opened up on the one on the right. Both went down quickly. I said "Let me ease outside the fence and glance back up the freeway." I stepped out and looked and didn't see anyone close. "All right, let's go collect their weapons and hightail it back to the blockade!"

We grabbed the RPG and the AK that they had and took off back to the barricade. We were twenty or so yards from the barricade and Morgan said "Hurry! Here comes a vehicle!"

We sprinted back. I handed Morgan the RPG and asked if anyone knew how to use it, he answered affirmatively and shouldered the weapon. "Don't stand behind me: It will make you a crispy critter." He got a solid rest on the barricade and said "OK, on my mark, open fire — but do not fire unless I do. It could still be civilians."

"Captain," I said, "There are no more civilians."

He looked at me and didn't say anything. The truck was closely followed by another vehicle with no headlights and they were building speed. The flashing lights on the barricade didn't seem to be causing any reason to slow down so you have to assume they had a different purpose in mind. At around 130 yards, the headlights switched to bright. The team put their hands up to shield their eyes and I said "You need to shoot now, Captain."

Before I could say "Captain," he sent the RPG for a direct hit in the grill of the first vehicle. It blew, and the second vehicle hit it from behind. The first vehicle exploded and rolled and the second vehicle slowed and swerved right to miss it. When it came out from behind the first truck, we let the second truck have it, with most of the fire concentrated on the windshield.

Then a nice little surprise happened as an armored NG vehicle pulled up and an M60 came online to hammer the second vehicle and then put an additional pounding on the first one. I said "Captain, that was a pleasant surprise. Do you have any others you might want us to know about?"

"Maybe later. Right now we need to go clean up that area."

Then a shout from the right side of the barricade said "There is a third vehicle!" When I looked back down the highway there it was, a small pickup traveling at a high rate of speed a couple hundred yards from us. Everyone trained their fire on the vehicle. It was nice having the M60, but the truck kept coming. I started shooting at the wheels hoping to blow tires and finally hit the left front and it blew out. The vehicle started swerving but was still coming. Someone else got the right front tire: Now there were sparks flying everywhere, because they were running on the rims.

Now it was within a hundred yards of us. Morgan told everyone to watch out and move to the sides, and watch the crossfire. We started scrambling to the sides behind the vehicles. The 60 kept pounding the little truck, which finally started slowing and started swerving even more, went sideways and rolled. The truck flipped twice and then exploded. The blast knocked most of us down and covered the center of the barricade in a fireball. It was good thinking for Morgan to send us to the sides of the barricade otherwise most of us would have been killed in that explosion.

As it turned out a couple of us had some minor burns and ringing in the ears. Morgan sent a three-man fire team down to check the casualties. I counted the number of National Guard troops and counted eleven, including the three that went to assess the casualties. I counted three police officers so the count was fifteen total: not a large force, but with these guys it felt like we were an army.

I asked Captain Morgan if I could speak with him, and we walked to the side of the barricade. "Captain, why do they seem to be so interested in blowing the barricade down here? I have been here all of about four hours and they have tried twice. It seems like they would be better served in establishing their operation inside the loop for a solid stronghold."

"We think there must be cells between the belt and where we are now. If they tried to go back into the city they would meet Kyle's team at the belt. My bet is the next thing they will try is a coordinated attack from this side and inside the loop to take out Kyle's team at the belt. So they really need to keep us busy so we can't reinforce them.

"Right now I have a team at the National Guard station on I-45 North of Texas City gearing up with some heavy vehicles. No tanks, but we are gearing up some transports with armor and M60s, and there is one 50 cal in the bunch. We will have an additional eight men when they get here, too, and also we are getting drones armed and up in the air setting a patrol grid to not only cover us but Kyle as well. Those will take time, they are not local and we have to bring them in from San Antonio, but once Ellington is back online we can operate from there. I do have some questions for you too—can you look at this map with me?"

"Sure. What do you need?"

"You told me you walked here from the beltway." "True."

"Can you show me the route you took?"

"Absolutely. I started here—" I pointed to the intersection of the beltway and Highway 3. "—and came down to here—" and pointed to El Dorado. "Then I moved over to I-45 and started south, staying in the fields on the west side. I was here when I intercepted the truck after the first attack."

"Do you think we could get the vehicles through those fields and stay out of sight?"

"It's possible. The fields out there are pretty big and they offer some cover. But I would recommend we go at night, if you have night vision. We may be spotted during the day. The area I would be most concerned about would be at El Dorado and I-45 on the southeast corner. There are a lot of apartments in that area and they are not known for an upstanding clientele. Look, from right here, we could get to highway 3 easily and then be on Highway 3 instead of passing directly in front of the apartments. Once we clear those, we don't need to cut fences and move into the fields. We can use the highway." I told him about the area around Ellington and asked if there was a security perimeter around it. He said there was a small contingent. "We should tell them we are coming by," I said.

"Do we have any drones up? So we could see where the guys are coming from that have hit us twice?"

"We didn't before, but we do now."

"Captain, how bad is this thing really? If we are getting this level of activity what is happening in other cities?"

"The intel I have says Houston is really being pounded, and there are armed militias moving through the city working on converts and killing civilian resistance. They have not moved outside the loop yet but they are building strength and probing the beltway forces to see what the resistance is like. Activity in Galveston has been almost nonexistent because of how hard it was hit by the chems and the fallout. Most everything there is rescue efforts by law enforcement." Again I got that sinking feeling and felt the need to get back there as soon as I could, but that wasn't going to happen for another day or two.

Morgan said he didn't have any information on DC or New York. I asked him if we had any intel on how successful ISIS was being in recruitment. He said "So far, it looks like the cartel and gang bangers are already on board, and so are some black radicals. However, it looks like the radical left, who have been building a quiet revolution in the country for years, may be emboldened enough to join in. Most of the civilian population is trying to stay low but it seems like they are getting bolder and more frustrated the longer the power stays off. Seems that the ISIS group is going around encouraging them to go take what they need from the surrounding stores, so they are starting to do that and once they get some momentum it becomes easy to just take what they want. Then when the local resources are gone, ISIS will have them expand the area they work. Like a swarm of ants, they'll start taking out other areas. You should probably get some rest. You'll be going with us to the beltway since you know the area."

"I kind of figured that," I said, and moved off the road to find a soft spot. Once I sat down and started thinking about everything that had happened to me over the last few days I started to get angry. Why is it that the people in this country could not see how much better our lives are than anyplace else in the world? Where else could you be where if you had the desire to work and build you could be as successful?

I started thinking back on how our country has changed over the last sixty years and it all became clear to me. First, create hypersensitivity about Political Correctness so that no one can say anything about what is happening without being called a racist or uncompromising, and you can protect the liberal agenda forever. ISIS and every other radical Muslim group has all of this figured out. They know that they can use the very things we are doing as weapons against us to bring us down. They saw the opportunity to send in their people during the open border era, they also use the political correctness front to make sure they are not discriminated against because of their color. The really sad part is that by the time our society wakes up to realize the only agenda ISIS has is that either you convert to Islam or you die, it may be too late. I can almost hear ISIS laughing at how stupid we are and that they have the opportunity they have wanted for a long time to destroy Christianity and the west. I prayed that people have not been dumbed down so much that they cannot see these things and we could turn this situation around quickly.

Now that they were here, they would move into the very areas that live off the welfare system and use them as cover for their operation. All they'd have to do is encourage them to go take what they need as if they were owed that. Once the shooting starts they would put them out front as human shields: brutal but effective.

It was midafternoon and I heard trucks coming, but these were coming from the south. I could see four vehicles: one transport and three light armored trucks. Looked like the good guys.

In front was one with a .50 cal, which was awesome. The second had an M60 mounted and the third was the transport followed by another one with an M60 on it. Morgan assigned vehicles, instructing the one that had been with us and three soldiers to stay and support the police at the barricade. He handed out some extra ammunition and gave the soldiers a few grenades as well. That put sixteen men in our four vehicles and four police and three soldiers at the barricade. The last thing Morgan said was "Stay sharp. We have no idea where the hot spots are right now, so we will take it easy."

In the lead vehicle there was a driver, a passenger side guy, me and one on the M60, the second vehicle had a driver, passenger and gunner. The best I know to describe the vehicles would be armored Humvee like things. The transport had a driver, a passenger and five in the back of the transport. The fourth and last vehicle had a driver and the gunner.

We started out headed north, taking our time and weaving around stalled vehicles. We drove slowly to highway 518 and turned back east. It was a few miles to highway 3, mostly through residential areas. We turned back north on Highway 3 and started moving toward Kyle's position at the beltway.

Going through the subdivisions, we had several people come out to the road and flag us down to ask if we had any updates on what was happening. We told them people are working on getting the power back on and to stay close to home. There should be some local emergency crews coming by soon to check on them. We didn't know if that was true or not but it seemed to make them feel better.

One person did tell us they heard some shooting close to Webster, the town we were headed to next.

Just before rolling into Webster, Captain Morgan got on the radio and told the team that there were reports of gunfire close, so stay frosty. We eased through town to take a look, and basically it was quiet. There did seem to be a lot of people out talking to each other and several of them waved us down to ask the status. We told them the same thing, but one of them said two trucks came through last night, shooting and trying to get people to come outside. Nobody did but they figured those would be back.

Then Morgan got a call on the radio. It was Kyle, who said "We have a big problem here—enemy combatants are setting up for an assault from the I- 45 area. It looks like they plan to hit us at dusk. I estimate about thirty-five to forty of them with weapons and we sure could use some help. Also, they have piled up cars on I-45 and you fellas won't be able to get through that way."

So Morgan turned to his team. "We need to roll, and now. So much for a stealthy entrance. We're rolling in as fast as we possibly can."

We told everybody to stay in their homes and we started up Highway 3 as fast as we could maneuver. About a mile from the beltway I told Morgan that the tree line on his left was the group of trees Kyle had been in. He radioed Kyle and told him we were close and would be coming up Highway 3. We could hear on the radio that things had started. We now heard gunfire coming from the highway ahead and knew things were getting ugly. Morgan pulled up some two hundred yards from the intersection of Highway 3 and the beltway and told the transport to unload and for the guys to move through the woods to a position behind Kyle—and to watch their fire, there were friendlies in there. Morgan radioed Kyle and said "We are coming in with five on foot from your rear and I will bring the vehicles up from 3 and turn south on the belt. We will have two vehicles go over to the south bound side and the rest will come in on the north bound side. Watch your fire."

"Understood."

The five on foot unloaded and headed into the trees and started making their way to the gunfire. I noticed it was easy to find folks when this was happening and you had two choices: either head toward the shooting or run away. These guys all ran to the shooting.

Our vehicles ran out onto the beltway and turned. One of the other armored vehicles pulled up in a wing position for us and the transport swung to the inside lane a little farther back. We pushed toward the fight.

Kyle came on the radio and said there were two vehicles with automatic weapons mounted on them coming over the overpass at that moment. Morgan said we saw them and instructed his gunners to take them out.

When the 50 lit up it was an awesome thing. The report and muzzle blast moved us around inside the vehicle but watching that thing work and following the tracers to see them hit the targets was impressive. Both vehicles were in flames in seconds. Then foot traffic was running all around the beltway and headed into the tree lines along the sides. A few went west into the trees. The remainder went east into the trees.

Morgan called Kyle and said "We will pull the 50 up to your position and have the two 60s set up on the west side of the road and start to move forward."

The five soldiers we sent in to Kyle's rear position were told to flank to the left and set up firing positions. When the roaches started running around some very concentrated and accurate fire was dropping them everywhere. The two vehicles with the 60s eased up a little and put more pressure on the enemy and they started to look really disorganized. Some ran out of the trees to run back to I-45 and started to pull back. The few that went west stayed in the woods on the west side. But this time we didn't let them just pull back.

Morgan said "All vehicles pursue, and the two on the west side set up watching the woods. Leave a rear guard of two on foot at Kyle's base and everyone else start a move toward I-45. Spread out through the woods to check for stragglers but do not go over the overpass, just clear the woods to the freeway. Once at the woods' edge, take up defensive positions and set up fire teams. And send a three man fire team to the north side of the woods and watch Highway 3."

Watching these guys do their jobs made me proud. The two vehicles on the west side of the belt had their weapons trained on the woods. There were still a few in there, but for the moment they were not shooting. I figured they were trying to regroup and I pictured them with eyes as wide as pie plates asking each other what just happened. Morgan told Corporal Walters to search the woods until they got to the tree line and set up defensive positions watching the freeway.

The two vehicles with the 60s on them on the west side of the belt moved into a fire-support positions to watch for anything moving through the woods. It was synchronized beauty.

Morgan asked Kyle to gather a three-man team and cross the belt to clear the woods on the west side. The team had been in the woods and working their way through them about ten minutes when I heard a small firefight break out: word over the radio was they'd contacted two hostiles. It ended quickly. The team called back that hostiles were down. There was one more short engagement about five minutes later and the word again was threat eliminated.

The team walked out at the end of the woods on the west side and Morgan told them to set up a line along the woods looking across I-45. Morgan ordered the transport and his vehicle with the 50 to move into the woods by Kyle's base camp. We parked close to Kyle's two vehicles.

Kyle walked into the camp area and looked at me. "Are those cowboy boots you're wearing?"

"It's a long story, and one that showed little or no compassion from friends."

"Aren't those my binocs?"

"No, I borrowed these from someone who used to be a friend."

"OK, then." We shook hands and I said it was really good to see him again and he said likewise.

Kyle and Morgan stood at the hood of the vehicle with the 50 cal on it and showed on the map where the team was deployed. It looked like they set up the majority of their team watching the freeway area and a couple facing where we had just come from to watch our backs. The vehicles were positioned in camp with gunners on point watching the beltway and in position to roll out to support the fire teams if needed. I noted that the rear area on the west side was not covered, so Kyle had his vehicle with the 60 on it move into the woods in that area.

Morgan said "I think we should put one of the 60s over here with the line watching across the freeway and the other over here watching the ramps." He pointed to the tree line just north of the belt intersection and then again just south at the ramps. "That way, anything coming over the freeway would have a lot of fire pointed at it. We have the 50 to roll out and cover anything coming in from the south if needed, or from the north on the beltway. The line of sight on the beltway is about two miles, and down Highway 3 is about a mile and a half." They agreed, and people were positioned. Then we settled in for a while and Morgan checked in with his team at the barricade.

The team at the barricade had enjoyed a few quiet hours and said things were good. They had seen limited traffic starting on the freeway and so far it was noneventful—mostly people from out of town who were curious to see what was going on.

Morgan put out a patrol to check out the casualties on the other side and to collect their weapons. That took about 45 minutes and when the team came back they reported there were ten down: Nine KIA and one wounded and being tended to. They had AKs and a couple of ARs along with one shotgun. Each one had some extra ammo so they were at least prepared for a conflict. Of the nine there was one white youth, three Hispanic and four black guys. All were young, about eighteen or so. The exception was a Middle Eastern guy who looked to be in his 20s, dressed in black. The others were dressed in casual wear, mostly blue jeans and t-shirts: nothing that in any way appeared to be uniform in appearance to say they were a unified fighting force.

So there I was, a full day later, and again it was getting dark and I was at Kyle's camp and moving away from Galveston instead of toward it. Some MREs were handed out, and some water so we "feasted" on dried meals and settled in for an evening of tense watching. Teams rotated in and out to get food and I got to hear their report of what activity they saw across the freeway. The reports sounded like they were assessing what happened and what would be a better game plan. No one believed the exchange was over yet and we all stayed on point in case we came under attack again.

Morgan answered a radio call and then told us the drone was on patrol above us now and they were collecting intel on what was going on. The reports said there was some activity but it seemed to be limited as far as how much outside time they spent, mostly they came and went from two buildings in the general area of where we went in to check the weapons stashes. I asked Morgan and Kyle if they thought there would be another attack. Morgan said "I am sure there will be, but they won't make the same mistake again. Now they know we have more firepower than they thought and they will try to come at us from the rear or sides where they have more cover and we should be the weakest."

Morgan told Kyle how to redirect his team, leaving a three-man fire team on each tree line watching the freeway. Then he repositioned his teams to cover the sides and back along Highway 3. Highway 3 also crossed under the belt and went on into Houston. Morgan said "We need a vehicle in the woods here," as he pointed to the woods on Highway 3 on the west side and a fire team for support. "That looks like a good place for them to come at us. They are not confident enough yet to move across the beltway very far south so they will come down the north side is my guess."

"We should count on a diversion. My guess is they will have a vehicle and a few troops come off the ramp and come at us from the front. Then their major push will be from the west side on Highway 3."

I asked if it might be time to move a scout team up on the ramp again and use the sniper to take out the diversion team before it got over the bridge. Morgan said :That would work. They would be confused, and anything we can do to add to the fog of war will help us."

I said "Well, I have been up there before and I can go as a lookout on the south side and maybe get some personnel counts as they cross the freeway. I would also suggest that the drone keep a close eye on the area across the freeway and move a little closer into Houston to see if they jump over to Highway 3 back up here somewhere and I pointed up 3 for a couple of miles. By now they have probably figured out we can see most of the area around the belt and I-45. I doubt they know about the drone yet." Morgan and Kyle agreed and Morgan redirected the surveillance of the drone to cover the areas we talked about.

I asked if they thought it would be a nighttime raid. Morgan and Kyle said they hadn't seen any night vision gear yet on these guys, but that didn't mean they might not have some. "If they attacked at night without it, they would be sitting ducks," said Morgan. "But if they think they might have the surprise of coming in on our back side they might try it."

I asked if they had an extra set of night vision goggles I could use up on the overpass. Kyle said "I only have one spare pair. Am I to assume it will be a loan like the binocs was?"

"I am not sure what you are talking about," I said. "I thought you issued those to a soldier."

"Maybe I did," he said with a grin.

We rested for a while, figuring the turds were licking their wounds and reforming a plan. Then I checked all my mags, tried on the night vision goggles and met up with the sniper and spotter again to get ready to move up the ramp.

I asked if I could trade my weapon for one with a sight that was better at night, and he took me to the transport and handed me an M4 with a scope that could light up the crosshairs when I pushed a button. That was cool. Kyle said "It will look different if you try to shoot with the goggles on. You need to try it out a few times to see if it will work, otherwise you may want to stay with open sights if you are not comfortable."

He showed me how to quickly remove the scope from the rail if I needed open sights. I asked Kyle if he had an extra pair of boots and he told me to check with Captain Morgan. Morgan said "I will get right on that."

I said "Man, I feel like I am back in High School." They both laughed.

We moved out to start up the ramp, low and slow. This time I felt a little safer because I knew there were fire teams watching the freeway and we should be clear to make our climb. We reached the top of the ramp that came from I-45 south and turned north on the belt and set up around the same cars we were at before. I started watching, first with the night vision to get a feel for them. I quickly realized that my distance vision was limited. But with the bright moon it actually seemed to work against long distance vision and I noticed it was bright but detail was difficult. So I took them off and went with the binocs.

Once my eyes had adjusted, I could see pretty well through them and could easily see any movement on pavement surfaces or areas that were lighter in color that worked like a backlight. The moon was bright and the binocs were great.

Then I remembered when I used to work for crisis hotline. The moon being full was the night nobody wanted to work because it got really weird.

CHAPTER 10:
WAIT FOR THE FLASH

I was in position watching the southbound side of I-45 from the overpass to Beltway 8. The roaches were out scurrying around tonight: I could see a lot of movement back on the west side of I-45 and there seemed to be a few crowds building around store fronts, looting most all of the stores.

I started getting an uneasy feeling that things were about to escalate when a fireball went up from a car that was set on fire. Then another shot, then another one and another car went up in a fireball. Now I could hear an occasional voice and started hearing more gunshots coming from the area west of I-45. Based on what I could see there were maybe two hundred people gathered in the area, and they were building in numbers.

I radioed back to Morgan and asked him what would be our tactic if we had a few hundred coming at us and most of them appeared to be civilian. He asked "Why? What are you seeing?"

"It looks like someone is really getting the locals riled up and they are starting to prepare to head our way."

Morgan said "OK, keep an eye on them, and keep me posted. If they move our way let me know immediately."

I said "No problem," and signed off. As I watched, there appeared to be a few who were inciting the crowd and telling them what to do. I radioed back to Morgan and asked "What if we took out the leaders who had weapons?"

He said "Hold on to that till we get a better idea of their intentions."

It didn't take long to know their intentions. They started moving as a group across the freeway to head toward the camp. I radioed Morgan and said "Here they come. It looks like two hundred or so about to move over the freeway and heading toward you."

Morgan said "Get out of there. Pull back immediately." We pulled up and headed out as fast as we could run to get back to the camp area.

Once back at the camp, Morgan said "The drone just relayed that a group of armed men were coming south on Highway 3 in two vehicles." He called in a drone strike on the two vehicles and we watched on his laptop as both were destroyed by a drone missile. We next saw a yellow fire ball go up about a mile from our position to the west. Morgan told his teams to stay ready and had another fire team moved to the beltway for additional fire power if we needed it. He ordered the vehicles out on the beltway so we now had three on the road. He had his teams up front along the tree line pull in to provide fire support as needed. I walked with Morgan and Kyle to the road and stood next to the vehicles as the group approached.

The group was shouting and waving things like tools, and a few had rifles. When they got to within about fifty yards, the vehicles hit the group with their high-beam headlights. They stopped and shaded their eyes with their hands for a brief couple of seconds. Morgan shouted for them not to come any closer, that we were US Military and we had fire teams on three sides of them. Then he asked who their spokesman was and what they wanted. Several shouts came from the crowd saying we had no right to be here, and they knew their rights. Morgan again said "Who is your spokesman? Send them out to talk."

Finally, a guy who I know I had seen on TV stepped out and walked toward us. He walked about ten yards and Morgan said "You can stop there," and started walking toward him. I started walking with Morgan. He looked at me and I thought he was going to tell me to stay put, but he didn't, so I kept walking.

Morgan introduced both of us and asked what his name was. He said his name was not important just what he had to say was. Morgan said "OK, Mr. Not Important what do you have to say?"

"You are killing our people and it has to stop."

"Your people? The ones with AKs that attacked us?"

"I don't know anything about that but if they did, they were defending themselves."

Morgan looked at me. "I'm a much better soldier than I am a diplomat. Do you want to try?"

"Sir," I said, "Do you know what has happened in the United States over the last four days?"

"What I know is we have no lights, no water and no help."

"No one else has those things either. Here is what has happened: A nuclear device was detonated in Texas City, one was detonated between Houston and Austin, others were detonated in Washington DC, Boston and in New York City's financial district. That knocked all the power out up and down most of the east coast. Terrorists are blowing up refineries, fuel storage tanks and now they are hitting soft targets like schools. Have you ever heard of a group named ISIS." He said he had. "They are the ones doing all of this."

"I don't believe you! They are the only ones helping us.

"What do you mean helping you?"

"Some of them have vehicles that run and they are helping us get food and water."

"Do you mean they are taking you to places to steal food and water?"

"It's not stealing if you need it to survive."

I glanced at Morgan and then I turned back to our detainee and asked "Do you know how they operate? First they create a major crisis, then they show up to point the blame at someone else. Then they encourage you to build resistance against the local authority. Once you start the process they then will take over the leadership of your group and start making laws on how it will operate. Next thing you know they will tell you that either you convert to Islam or you will die that it is the only way to purge the corrupt society you live in."

"Ain't nobody gonna tell me what I can and can't do!"

"Remember you told me that when they shoot your neighbor or behead a friend of yours. Captain Morgan, I don't think I am helping here."

Morgan asked him, "Sir, what are your intentions with this group?"

"I told you, we are here to tell you to leave."

"I can't do that sir. We are in a state of war and martial law has been declared. I recommend that you take these people back to their homes right now so we don't have any trouble and no one gets hurt. I have troops in the woods on both sides of you and they are heavily armed. We are prepared to die tonight following our orders. Are you willing to die tonight too? Is the group with you willing to die also? Because once it starts, we will finish it in a big way. I recommend you turn around and go tell the people with you that it is better that you all go home right now."

The guy looked him up and down and turned slowly to go back, then he stopped. He turned around and said "This ain't over" and kept walking.

I looked at Morgan and said "I was afraid he would say that."

We walked back to the vehicles and watched to see what they were going to do. Instead of going home the crowd got louder and angrier. I said "Well, I guess he didn't have any other choice. He got them in the mood for a fight, and now whether he wants it or not it may just happen. I think that in a lot of cases the activist is doing what he does to stir things up, and then unfortunately events take their own course and lots of people get hurt. There is always the potential for disaster when you burn trash during a drought."

We all stood next to the vehicles to give us some cover in case someone started shooting, and sure enough they did. First came a Molotov cocktail, then several shots rang out. Morgan told his team to hold their fire. Then another cocktail came in, this one a little bit closer to us. Again Morgan said "Hold your fire! Gunners, I want you to lay down some fire at that group of trees over there where we do not have any troops on my command." A few more shots rang out and he said "Now!"

The night lit up when the gunners opened up. No one in the crowd was targeted but they all turned and ran back across the freeway overpass. I bet a few of them had to change their britches when they got home.

He said "I didn't think they had a reason to fight, but they needed to make a showing."

I said "Now what I fear is once they get back they will start talking it up and the next time they will come to fight."

"I know, but maybe we saved a few lives tonight because I don't think all of them will come back a second time."

Morgan redeployed his troops to cover the back and sides again and we pulled the vehicles off the road into our camp area. This time Morgan had Kyle put together a patrol to cruise up and down the side of the roadway and a vehicle in the road to show we were still there. He also had them roll back up Highway 3 to check on the vehicles the drone took out. After checking on the burned-out vehicles, the soldiers came back and said it looked like there'd been about five in each vehicle, and all were KIA.

We settled in to try and get some rest with guys rotating watches. I volunteered to take a watch but it didn't start until 3 AM so I piled up against a tree and went to sleep. At 2:45 I was nudged and told it was my watch and I was to go to the southeast tree line and relieve one of the soldiers.

When I got there I asked if there had been any activity and he said only a little foot traffic not much to speak of. My team mate was a soldier named Collins, who looked so young I figured him to be maybe eighteen or nineteen. So I asked the usual get-to-know-you questions like *where are you from, do you have a family, are you married, any kids,* that kind of stuff.

At daylight I was relieved by a soldier and went back to base camp. Morgan was there getting debriefed by his teams. I waited for him to finish and he walked over to where I was by the transport and said "It looks like you may be able to get into Galveston today. You still want to go?" "Yes, sir." "OK. Follow me."

We walked to one of the armored vehicles and he said "You'll go with these guys back to the barricade. The barricade had two more probes tonight and they will need some reinforcement."

"That sounds good. Thank you for thinking about me."

I asked Morgan "Before we leave, can I have a word with you?" We both moved off to the side I started by saying "First I want to thank you for taking care of me the last couple of days." Morgan said "You pulled your weight around here, so thank you for your service."

"Captain, have you heard anything about what is happening in other parts of the city?"

"I have heard that it is much worse in some other areas. The areas around the belt and 59 are heavily engaged. Our guys are set up in the old shopping mall at the corner of 59 and Bissonnett. They have steady fire coming in from the street side and an occasional intrusion from behind, but so far they are holding their own. Also the area around the belt and I-45 north are in a similar situation."

"Do you have any idea how coordinated the groups fighting seem to be?"

"So far they just seem to be testing our capabilities and have not put a concerted effort into a move that we have seen. Downtown has not been checked out very much because it has been too hard for us to get inside the beltway. We are not sure what the status is in there. But once we get reinforcements we should be able to start going in to see what is happening. All we know is there is a lot of gunfire around the city and we suspect that it is individuals who are fighting back."

"That makes sense. There are lots of guns in Texas. Captain, do you have a status from Galveston?"

"The chems are clear but we don't have any final casualty counts yet—but the preliminary estimate is really high. Most of the casualties are in the downtown area and eastern parts of the island. It looks like the far western parts of the island seemed to do pretty well. That's all I know."

"Captain Morgan, how bad do you think this could get, and how prepared are the response teams for the problem?"

"Right now it isn't looking good and it could get really ugly. Most of our true combat troops are overseas or have left the service so we are working with a smaller military than we had just four years ago. The reductions by our government in the budget and the de-emphasis of military by the current administration have us at a disadvantage for fighting a war. It will take time to rebuild our forces and get in position to take the trouble spots back. As for chemical response, we have taken the stance it won't happen here for the last seven years.

"Currently, the stepped-up attacks on our forces around the world have made it difficult for us to pull back quickly to defend our internal structure. We pull back and we lose all of the other areas of the world we have fought to hold off terrorism and then the areas we have to take back are even bigger and more of a problem than before. But if we don't pull back we could lose the country from within and that solves nothing. Either way, the US loses.

"Politicians allow jihadists to come over our borders just so they can bring in voters who will keep them in office. I have to admit, the plan was brilliant and very well thought out. But I don't think any of the vote-seeking politicians expected the radical Islamists to use their plan to take out all of us. But I could be wrong—maybe they are working together, and I am a fool! My greatest fear is with the US made completely dysfunctional by all of this, what could happen to the world without us to keep this kind of evil in check? We have taken such a 'look the other way' approach with these guys that we have created the perfect environment for them to recruit and grow.

"Our administration decided to make a show of fighting by sending air support into Iraq and Syria to bomb the ISIS group, but we only succeeded in scattering the roaches. Without boots on the ground, we didn't do anything but stir up the hornet's nest. Once the US didn't show a strong approach, the other countries of the world decided they were not going to put boots on the ground if the US didn't. The whole thing might have looked good in the press for a few months but it did nothing to stop the problem. Instead it shifted the focus to the US."

"It is scary but I'll do my job and I know my troops will too. There is always hope in the American spirit and you see it in the hearts of these young men who fight for truth and freedom. I shook Morgan's hand and then looked for Kyle so I could say bye but he was on the line somewhere. I climbed in the vehicle with three other soldiers and we started south on Highway 3.

CHAPTER 11:
HEADED SOUTH, FINALLY

We turned out on Highway 3 with our gunner swinging the 60 back and forth while watching the sides of the road. A glow was just starting on the horizon to our left as we pulled out. We took our time, neither going fast nor going slow. It was a cautious movement as we drove down Highway 3. We went past El Dorado and on to 646 before turning back to I-45.

Once on I-45 we started north with no headlights and moving very deliberately. Within a mile or so of the barricade we radioed the team we were coming in and turned on our headlights. Just before we got to the barricade, we turned off our lights to help stop night blindness and pulled the vehicle into a defensive position on the other side of the barricade.

I stepped down out of the vehicle and said my hello to everyone and then asked the guys how they were doing and what the incursions had been like. In both cases they said the trucks pulled up about 300 yards from them and just sat there. On one occasion, they started up and drove fast at the barricade but stopped short and turned around. I said "Sounds like they're probing you to see how you react. I used to see that in airports and public landmarks all the time when I worked at DHS."

I asked if they knew of anyone going into Galveston that I might be able to catch a ride with. One of the police officers got on the radio and found an emergency vehicle that was transporting casualties back and forth from Galveston and asked if I could ride with them down to the island. They agreed and my ride pulled up in about forty-five minutes. I climbed in the back of the ambulance and took a seat with two EMS guys and we started south.

While we were traveling I asked them what they were seeing on the island. Both were very quiet and seemed to be a little overwhelmed with what had been happening but one of them said "So far, we have only transported the ones who are alive. The count has been about 300. The ones that are dead are still there and are being removed by other teams."

I asked them what areas they had been in on the island and they said it was the area mostly east of 61st Street. It looked like Bolivar was spared but the area from 61st to the end of the seawall was hard hit. They said tanks with cyanide at one of the plants ruptured and that was what floated over the island. I noticed that there were more cars on the road so I asked one of the EMS techs and he said that the EMP wasn't as effective on the island because of the distance and curvature of the earth.

I asked if they had made any runs to Tiki and they said no. The local team on Tiki had been handling that mostly. I asked them if there had been any looting or problems from terror events such as bombings and they said not the island but they had heard reports from other areas and knew it was happening. I asked them if they felt like this was all a coordinated attack and each one said it absolutely felt that way.

The driver slowed as we pulled up on the Tiki exit, which is just before the causeway, and let me out. I thanked them and started walking into the entrance. There was a police barricade there and they were a little disturbed that I was carrying a weapon, so I held it over my head and told them who I was and that I lived on the island and wanted to check on my wife.

I noticed that they were not just carrying their standard side arms but also had tactical weapons handy. I briefed the officers on my events over the last few days and how the EMP impacted areas were in turmoil, with plenty of weapons and attacks on National Guard troops and police going on back up the freeway. I told them everything from my walk from the Woodlands to the barricade events back up on I-45.

I asked them if there had been any casualties on Tiki, he said some were sick from the chems and two elderly had died. I asked if the island had been evacuated, they said yes but some decided to stay and they couldn't force them to leave—just recommended it highly.

I told them I wanted to walk in to my house and see if my wife was OK, they said "You can, but odds are she is not there."

I asked if they had a list of the ones taken to the hospital and they said they didn't have one yet. I also said "If she is not there I will be back through here at some point. Is the electricity on?"

"Not yet. The grid's still down, but it could be back on in a day or two." I started walking. It was about two miles to our house since we lived on the end of the island.

As I made the turn on our street and I could see the house, I noticed my wife's car was not there. I hoped it was because she left in it but the way things had gone over the last five days, anything could have happened. As I walked in the driveway I checked my weapons, figuring that if she was not there, the house should be empty, but better safe than sorry. Our house is on twelve-foot stilts, as are most new houses on the coast, so I went up the side stairs to see in the back of the house before I entered through the front. Once convinced the house was clear I had to go back down the side steps and enter through the front steps because

I didn't have my back-door key with me. There was no movement and no one I could see. Once inside, I did a check of all the rooms. There was no one there. The dogs, two Labradors and a cat were gone too, so my bet was they were with my wife.

I wasn't sure yet where I was going but I felt like I needed to be prepared. Then I saw the note on the counter. It was from her.

She said she had no idea if I was OK, but she was going to try and make it to my daughter's house, and she thought she had enough gas to get there. That was a huge relief. At least she made it out of there! My hope was she was able to get rolling before the areas got bad, and she made it safely. I checked the cabinet where she kept a .357, and it was gone. It was good she had enough foresight to take that with her. That made me feel just a little better, but a woman alone in a car would still be an easy target.

Nothing felt right, since I was preparing for a fight with an enemy whose plans I could only guess about and I was headed somewhere I hadn't figured out yet. If my wife was at my daughter's house, that meant I had to go back the way I had just come from and this time move more west than north to get there. That would take me right through some of the worst areas around 59 and Bissonnett that Morgan had said was heavily engaged with the National Guard. That was not what I wanted to do right now. To go around those areas meant another five or six days on foot, unless I could find a vehicle.

I found a few things to eat in the pantry and walked out on the deck to sit down for a few minutes. I really needed to build a plan.

I sat in one of the rocking chairs and stared across the bay to regroup and started reflecting on what had happened. There was one boat but it appeared to be Coast Guard auxiliary. I walked back in the house and sat in my recliner; the M4 was still in my lap. I didn't even know it when I went to sleep. I woke up around five hours later.

When I tried to stand up I realized I was so sore I almost couldn't move. My overweight old body had not been in this kind of a mess in a long time. I stretched to try and get some mobility back and walked stiff legged to the pantry to eat some dry cereal. I did notice the way my pants and shirt were fitting now, so all this exercise had one positive thing going for it.

I went back out on the deck to sit and think about what I should do next. I was trying to decide if I wanted to try and get to my daughter's house and how I might be able to run a route that took me the long way around but would let me miss the really bad spots on the belt. My suspicion was that if those areas around the belt were having trouble, the loop and inside of it must be a total mess.

The longer I sat there the madder I got. Everything about who my enemy was and what they were doing kept working deeper and deeper into my soul. Then I thought about those guys I had just been with and how thin they were stretched and how I wondered if I could help them. That was when I decided I was going back and see if they wanted my help at the barricade or wherever.

Inside my closet in a spare bedroom I kept my hunting clothes, and my guns were in the safe. A couple of years ago I hunted mule deer in west Texas, and the best camo for that part of the state was digital camo or the Army's Universal Camo Pattern. I found a full set online and had them hanging in my closet. I also finally could get a good pair of walking boots. I found out the water was running because of a generator at the water plant so I showered and refreshed to the point where I felt human again. I also threw a couple deodorants into my pack.

I went through my gun safe and pulled out my tactical shotgun, a Mossberg 590. I grabbed my .45 XD and the leg holster. I spent the next couple of hours putting together a pack with ammo and necessities. Once I had myself outfitted with what I thought I might need, I went downstairs to see if there was any food that I may be able to take along.

I noticed my Khukuri knives on the mantle. I decided that one would be handy if I needed to go through brush or good in a pinch if I needed a weapon. I looked in the mirror and it was clear what I was going to do: I was going to fight with our soldiers, if they would have me.

I thought to myself that if we were able to get some of the areas back under control then it would be easier to work my way over to my daughters house and I wouldn't have to walk another 70 miles. I went over to the note my wife left me and began to write a response so she knew that I have been here. "I think you went to Lindsay's, and I hope you made it. If you are reading this it means you have come back home and things are stable here. Keep your gun loaded and be vigilant. I am going to meet up with the National Guard if they will take me and take back our state. After that I am not sure. If I don't come back, I am sorry, but it is what I need to do. I want you to know I love you and I am doing this so we can live in peace. Remember this, Texas will not fall easily. We will show these guys a few things. I will either see you at Lindsay's house or back here someday. I love you."

So, with a heavy backpack and several weapons, I locked the house and started walking back to the bridge that led onto the island. As I approached the roadblock by the local police, they said "You look different." I said "I feel different, too."

The police asked me if she was there and I said "No, and the car was gone so I hoped she got out safely."

"She probably did. We told people to leave immediately and to go around Highway 6 to the west instead of going north on I-45 if they were headed west or north."

"Good idea! Thanks for doing that. Have you been having any problems?"

"No, it's been pretty quiet."

"Do you think I might hitch a ride back to the barricade with an emergency vehicle?" The Lieutenant responded by getting on the radio and asking if anyone was headed out, then told me that he would have me over on the northbound side of the road so they didn't have to detour to pick me up. He said he would get a call back when one was coming, and he said "Hop in my car and I'll take you over to the other side of the freeway."

While waiting for the EMS to come over the causeway he asked me what I was going to do. I said "I am going back to help the National Guard at the barricade and anywhere else they need me."

"Well, good luck to you." I got out of his car just on the downhill side of the causeway, an easy place for the EMS to stop. I thanked him for the ride and he shook my hand and pulled away.

Over the causeway came the EMS. They slowed and pulled up to me, and I climbed in. "Hey soldier, where you headed?" "Headed to the barricade or as close as you can get me on I-45." The driver said no problem and we rolled out with the lights on at about eighty-five miles an hour. It took twenty minutes to get to the barricade, and when I stepped out of the vehicle the guys recognized me and said "Look who is back!"

I asked them if the food had improved any and they said "You bet, every day is a banquet."

"Well, at least now I have a good pair of boots. I figured that if I was going to hang out with you guys I needed some camo or I might as well just paint a bull's eye on my shirt." That was when I realized that Sergeant Kyle was there with the group and their numbers had grown a little. I said "Kyle I see you are still alive."

"Yep. Each day I wake up on the green side of grass it's good. I see you have lost some weight. Looks like the Army life has been good to you."

I laughed. "Yep! Where else can you get all of this sunshine, exercise and great food? It's better than the fat farm."

I asked Kyle "Can I help in any way? I think I need to be here, this is my country too."

"Well, we can always use the help."

I looked at Kyle and said "I guess I'm in the Army now."

He laughed and said "Well you could still fail the physical." I laughed and sat down behind the barricade.

I said "I have already done that once, in 1973, because of a sports injury." Kyle asked what I found in Galveston, and I told him the story of the note and how I hoped my wife got out and was at my daughter's house. He said he hoped so too.

I asked Kyle what it had been like on the beltway and he said "I just got word some crews are going to attempt to repair some of the grid stations and need our support for cover. It is in the area along the coast and we don't expect a lot of problem there. The activity in the area has expanded and we've had to set up a perimeter around the storage tanks along the belt for Ellington and the refineries just up the road. Those have had to be reinforced twice and now the team was up to about 70 troops spread out all along the belt from I-45 to I-10."

"Kyle, show me where the power team escorts are going and maybe I can give some advice." He picked up his map, pointed to an area around Clear Lake, and said "Here's where we're going. Tell me what you know about these areas." I told Kyle about the areas I thought might be troublesome and mapped a route for them to travel that would skirt the problem areas.

Kyle also said Morgan was engaged along refinery row on Highway 225 almost constantly, and he figured that reinforcements would be coming Morgan's way pretty soon. The problem was he wasn't sure where they would come from, it seems that the National

Guard is almost tapped out and we are pulling up everyone we have, and it may not be enough for a security force, much less to form an offensive team to clear these radicals out. By ISIS stirring it up on all sides of the beltway they have our forces spread in a loop nearly 150 miles long. That is too long a line to hold with the troops we have. It is like guarding the border of a small country.

I told Kyle "I've been thinking about how I can best support you guys, and I think that if I can build a coalition of Texas fighters to support you, we could solve our problems."

"What do you mean?"

"If I can create a Texas militia that is formed from former military people we could have a formidable army to support you guys. We could hold the line on the perimeter and you all could start cleaning up this mess. Of course we would follow your orders but we could fight and together we could take back Houston and then Texas. I believe that Texas has a mind-set that nobody is going to do this to us, and we could build a fighting force that would do better than the one at the Alamo— after all, the guys in the Alamo were outnumbered twenty to one! But it will need to be focused and not just out there fighting, it needs to have a goal in mind and meet the objectives we set for overall victory.

"I would use CB and ham radio to recruit people from the areas. If we told them we would have someone at the county courthouses in each county to sign them up and give them orders we could have an Army in a few weeks. I doubt that ISIS will be monitoring the ham radio frequencies initially and we would have some time to build a fighting force before they figured out what was happening. I also believe to do that, we need a solid plan of how to coordinate the resources and make sure we all work together. I can go into the neighborhoods that I believe are middle class and build a fighting force that can retake Texas and get this scum out of our area."

"You need to talk to Morgan."

"Then get me to Morgan so I can throw the idea at him and start building a strategy." Kyle looked around and said to a private whose name was Stills, "Get your gear and two troops and take this man to Morgan. You leave in fifteen minutes."

CHAPTER 12:
YOU'RE IN TEXAS NOW—
DON'T MESS WITH US

Kyle had me on the ride to Morgan's camp in fifteen minutes, just like he said. Now that I was rolling and knew I had at least twenty five minutes to reflect I started thinking about what I had said to Kyle and whether it was really something I could accomplish. Was the timing right for a militia? So much had to be determined as far as the amount of impact these rebel groups were having. It may have been early, but I figured that with the amount of time it would take to train and have a viable fighting force, we should start planning as soon as possible in the event we needed it. It was a big task to get people to come together and fight for a cause much less to do it in a coordinated fashion.

Could I actually do what I said I could do? Could I get an army from the people in Texas to fight the Islamic terror group trying to take our state and our country? I figured if I could get the folks in Texas to first of all understand what was happening and then to get angry enough to fight back, then we could clear Texas and have it reestablished as sovereign, and then we could worry about the rest of the country.

First reclaim Texas. Then we worry about everything else.

While driving, I started looking for radio towers and anything that could lead me to where I might get communications out to the general public in Texas. I had to assume that electricity and communications might not be back on for a while, so I needed alternative solutions. I made note of what looked like middle-class neighborhoods and any area where I felt like former military staff might be living.

I began to think about the VHF radio in my boat and how the working class listened to these frequencies and how they were a different group of people who didn't tolerate the kind of garbage we were seeing. They may be silent when it comes to being on the news but they had strong convictions and they would pick up a weapon and let you know in a very direct way if their freedom was threatened. They would fight, but they needed to know it was for something, and that it would end sometime, and they would know they were fighting for an end game and it had to a cause that they believed in. They needed to know there was a clear victory set for them.

Were they fighting for their way of life? Were they fighting for their own personal freedom? Or were they fighting for the government they now believed was corrupt and which they did not support? I had to make sure they knew they were fighting for Texas and their own individual freedom as well as their family.

I started looking at a map and built a plan of neighborhoods I would go into to start recruiting an army. I figured that first of all we needed to build a strong resistance so that the neighborhood they lived in would be secure and could resist any incursion short of a full assault that might occur. You don't want them to leave their neighborhoods to fight only to have their homes fall. Then I would instruct them to select the best warriors they had and send them to a meeting location at several designated safe points around and outside the beltway. Then we could integrate them into the overall army of Texas. The Texas Army would then be subject to the overall National Guard of Texas under the direction of the Governor and be used to fight against ISIS and any forces that threatened Texas.

I started to second-guess my own boldness, and now my biggest problem was self-confidence. How do we train these people once we get them? How do we show them we have a plan and they are part of a vision? They will need to be able to be a fighting force that would be effective and not give their lives unnecessarily. I needed to have expert military training for a militia, which was what we have been doing in the Middle East. Can we do it in Texas?

I needed to talk to Morgan, I trusted him to tell me what was available and how I could put it together in a solid plan. Then I asked myself if I was the guy to do this: Am I taking on something bigger than I was able to complete? Can I pull this together? I don't know, maybe, but at the moment there wasn't anyone else to get it done and the time was now. I had to do this now or lose everything I hold dear.

We made the exit off of the beltway at the I-10 feeder and went into the area where Morgan had established his camp. As we pulled in, several troops came out to meet us and showed us where to park. I noticed that Morgan's team had grown some and now there were at least twenty at camp as support troops. As we pulled into camp I stepped out of the vehicle and Morgan met me and said "Hello soldier. I see you got a pair of boots to wear."

"Yes sir! No thanks to the US Government—these are mine!"

He laughed and said "Those are the best kind! They always fit better."

I updated Morgan on all that had happened to me over the last few days and told him my resolution about fighting until our problems were solved. He said he was glad to have me back and that he could always use a good consultant.

"Thanks. You should know how much I respect what he stand for and what they do."

"Okay, just stop with all the butt kissing. Why are you really here?"

I laughed and said "Well, the reason I came looking for you is because you work like I do: direct and to the point. And the food is good. But here's the thing. Do you think if I could find a volunteer army that would stand your positions on the belt so you can form a plan to clear out the problem areas would you be interested?"

"Maybe. Maybe. What are you thinking?"

I told him about my evangelism campaign and how I would go into the neighborhoods I believed would be good recruiting grounds and start gathering an army. I told him it was likely there could be a large number of former military and that the team would not be a bunch of rednecks with guns but people who have fought before and understand some discipline. I told him I would continue recruiting and as they cleared areas we would move in behind them to establish a safe zone.

I told him my biggest problem would be logistics: how to feed them and how to keep them supplied with essentials like ammo and vehicles. Morgan said "That's our problem right now too, but we expect to get some help from other states soon. We may get some help in the next couple of weeks."

"I couldn't get a very big team collected by then anyway. My biggest issue is communications so I have been thinking about how I may be able to do that. Do you have access to any more generators?"

"I can get a few. Why?"

"If we found ham radio operators in key areas, we could use the airwaves to communicate back and forth. I doubt that ISIS has CB or ham monitored yet. We could keep the military channels clear by using the ham operators and all we would need is military coordination information to relay to the central communications team and it would go out on the radio."

Morgan put his map on the hood of his vehicle and said "Show me how you would do this."

"First, I would start by working these areas south of town in the middle and upper middle class areas south of Houston. If the grid to the east is coming online to provide power to the southern areas first we will need to make sure they stay safe and secure. By getting them online we could also reduce the strain on your team to escort the power companies they would know they are going into safe zones. I think that would speed up the repairs a great deal."

I pointed to some neighborhoods east of Houston and said "I would move into these neighborhoods so we could help secure the refinery area. I don't think we will be ready to take them over completely for a while but we could reinforce your teams there. The refinery row area like the one we are in now must be protected or it could take years to rebuild. Once the south and east are secured we would move back to the west, but to go west I will need to recruit in the northwest areas here—" I pointed on the map to a large area of middle class neighborhoods. "—Then we will make our move to the west and we can use some resources from recruiting in the southern areas and northwest. I think the best recruiting areas will be south and northwest. I am really worried about the area southwest. How bad has that area been?"

"Really bad. The looting is off the charts and our teams there have been under almost constant small arms fire. The area southwest and due west are under Major Henson. He is in charge over there. The area north is Captain Steel. I have the south and east areas. But we all report to Major Henson. Henson reports to a colonel in a command post somewhere to the west of Houston: His name is Birdwell."

I said "My feeling is that the areas north and southwest will have the heaviest resistance because of the neighborhoods inside the belt. Recruiting will be really hard unless I go farther outside the beltway in both of those areas. I said there are no strategic targets in those areas but there are plenty of soft targets and my guess is these guys will blow up soft targets just because they like it. As always, my first objective would be to form a neighborhood protection team and then bring recruits with us to secure the beltway areas. My preference will be to only bring former military to the beltway and leave the other volunteers in the neighborhoods because anyone will fight if their family is threatened."

Morgan said "OK, that could be a plan, but now we have to go see Henson. Then he may want us to go with him to see Birdwell. He has to approve it before we do anything else. Saddle up! This ride could be hairy." So. My first move was to get an MRE and some water and check all of my mags to make sure I had what I needed.

Morgan had an armored vehicle with a 60 on top getting ready. He also added four troopers to our team and we started west on the beltway. I felt tense because Morgan had said it could be "hairy," but I also had worked in the area we were going into and I knew it was one of the highest crime rate areas in the city. It also had several mosques in the immediate area and that didn't bode well for unrest.

The trip from I-45 to just past 288 was not a problem, but as we drew closer to Highway 90, I noticed the driver started to slow and be a lot more deliberate in his focus. Morgan went on alert once we crossed the Highway 90 overpass and instructed the gunner to be sharp and for everyone to watch for movement on all sides. He also said for us to watch for IEDs on the side of the road. That was scary: I wouldn't know what an IED looked like and I would be a greasy spot on the road by the time I figured out what it was. I asked Morgan what to watch for, and he said to look for fresh dirt where there has been digging, or for anything lying alongside or in the road. He said one of our biggest problems is the stalled cars. Morgan said "They have been putting bombs in them and detonating when we go by. So far their timing sucks, because we vary our speeds a lot when we go around them so they are having trouble timing things. But they could still get lucky. Even a blind hog finds an acorn sometimes."

I noticed that as we got closer to US 59 there seemed to be more burned cars on the freeway than in the areas we had just come through. There was smoke coming from the area inside the belt close to 59 and it there were at least five fires I could see. Over to the west and slightly south there were another five or six fires going. Morgan looked back at me and said "Henson's command post is back southwest on 59 about four miles."

"That is out past Highway 6. There used to be some great places to eat Cajun food in that area but I probably wouldn't go there right now." On the overpass going from the belt to Highway 59 I noticed there were several cars set up to block our exit so it meant we had to get off on the feeder and go under the freeway. That would be a great place for an ambush, but as we made the exit I saw a patrol set up there to stop that exact thing. I breathed a sigh of relief. These guys were good.

Morgan said "The worst is just ahead of us. From the belt to Highway 6 our teams have been taking fire frequently. Just stay alert and be ready if we have to return fire. For now we are just going to try and run through it without having to engage." As he said that I heard rounds hitting the vehicle, and out in front of us a handful ran to cover around some stalled cars and opened up on us. They had AKs, but they were semi auto, not military issue with full auto. The gunner on the 60 returned fire…and man, did he ever return fire! He started chewing up vehicles and had the roaches running.

Two didn't make it out of their cover, as that they had not figured out that a high-velocity .30 caliber round will go through both car doors and the only way to get cover is to stay behind the wheels. Too bad for them... but after all, they started it.

We made it to Henson's camp in under seven minutes after the engagement at the parked cars. Once we pulled in, Morgan had his vehicle and his gunner set up to add support for Henson's team, also supported by Captain Sanchez, who was with Henson when we pulled up. Morgan turned to me and said "Let me do the talking to set the stage for you. Then tell Henson exactly the same things you told me, say 'yessir' a lot and be direct and to the point. I have the map, explain your ideas and use the map just like you did with me."

"Got it. Any other suggestions?"

"Nope, just stay cool and present this plan like you know how it will happen."

"But what if I don't know for sure it will work?"

"Then we might as well go back right now."

I thought about it for a minute or so. "OK, let's go. This has to work, or our country will be in an internal war for the next hundred years."

Henson was a medium height, lean and mean, steely eyed guy who Morgan said had fought in Iraq and Afghanistan. This was not his first rodeo with terrorists and he clearly had a mission to destroy them. He was also very familiar with house-to-house fighting tactics and knew what he was up against. Morgan told me he was from Dallas, so that doubled his credibility with me, as did his attitude about these dirtbags.

Morgan saluted and said "Captain Morgan, sir: requesting a few minutes of your time."

Henson saluted back and said "What I can do for you, Captain?"

"Colonel, this man is Will Terrell. He has been helping us as a consultant for the past couple of weeks because he knows the city really well. He is also a good common sense guy who's put some pretty good ideas out there for us to work with. His information has helped us a great deal and he is also pretty good in a fight, sir—he has covered my back a couple of times now and has proven to be valuable to us. He has some ideas I wanted to get to you that I think could help us, sir."

Henson looked me dead in the eyes and said "What ideas, Mr. Terrell?"

"Captain Morgan, would you like to lead, or do you want me to start?"

"Go for it, Terrell."

I told Henson the entire plan using Morgan's map exactly the way I explained it to Morgan. Henson listened intently and never said a word. After I finished I looked at Henson, but he was fixed on the map, so I waited for what seemed like an eternity, and he still didn't say anything. All of a sudden I felt stupid and that my idea was ludicrous. Then Henson looked at me and said "What will you need to do this?"

I almost fainted, then I stuttered a little bit and said "Well, sir, a couple of vehicles and some escort troops would be nice. Also as many generators as you can get your hands on. I need at least five plus a remote gas tank to put in each secured neighborhood. I may need to equip some of the militia with arms but my bet is a lot of these guys will have their own weapons. For now, I will go with 'bring your own gun' and if we need to step up the firepower I will get back with you."

Henson looked at me and asked "Do you really think you can do this?"

"Yes sir. I have lived in Texas my whole life and we are really pissed off right now."

Henson turned to Morgan and Sanchez and said "Get this man what he needs. Mr. Terrell, you will report to Captain Morgan and you need to keep him informed every step of the way. Do not hold back any intel you collect no matter how small or insignificant you may think it is. I will expect a status report every day on your progress and how many recruits you have been able to gather."

"Colonel, there is one more thing: We will need some training, so that we are focused and not just running around with guns. I will set up designated areas for recruits to gather so it will be easier to train them."

Henson said "I agree. I will get Special Forces to contact you and provide your teams with training... but, Mr. Terrell, you would be better off training in small groups so you do not draw attention to large groups gathering. You will need to adjust your plans accordingly. It means more tactical coordination, but you will save a lot of lives doing it that way."

"Yes, sir. Duly noted."

Henson said to Morgan "I expect to see where your communications points are and when they come on line with an area of coverage as soon as possible."

I said "Colonel there is a list of registered ham operators in our area. They typically register in a group so that they know who is out there." To Henson I said "If you could get a list of the operators and their addresses, it would shorten our search time tremendously."

"I can do that, and I will have it for you tomorrow." Henson looked at Sanchez and left the room to start finding the information.

Henson said "You guys should get something to eat, and relax while we gather the resources and information you need. I can get you the vehicles but Morgan will have to help with the troops. I am really spread thin here."

Morgan said "Yes sir, we will cover the escort staff."

"We will try to get you rolling as soon as possible. Mr. Terrell, we have to stop what is going on in this city. If we don't do it soon, we may not be able to get it back without a lot of lives being lost."

Morgan saluted and so did I because I really didn't know how to end the conversation, and then Henson saluted back and we turned and walked out.

As we stepped out of Henson's tent I looked at Morgan and said "Well, now I have to do what I promised."

"Yep. I hope you can do this, because now I am on the island with you."

"Yep, and I think I just set the ship on fire and pushed it off. Looks like we are here to stay."

Morgan looked at me and said "I don't even know you all that well." From the tent we heard Henson say "I have a feeling that may be changing."

Morgan and I walked to the mess area, a name I always considered weird for a place to get food. But it was good to be at HQ. They had warmed over stew and a piece of bread with it, but I did get a glass of tea which tasted great. I sat with Morgan and looked him in the eyes and said "Now I'm worried. I have to deliver on what I put out there. Do you think I can get this done?"

"I do, and I think you believe you can do it too, so shut up and eat."

We had just finished eating when a corporal came up to us and saluted. "Captain Morgan we have your vehicles ready for you."

Morgan saluted back and said "Thank you, Corporal, we will meet up with you in a few minutes." He looked me in the eyes. "Terrell just to set the record straight, I know you can do this and I have your back. So let's get going and make these turds pay for what they are doing in our country."

"Let's start with our state first, and then we will move to the rest of the country." He grinned and said "Agreed!"

When we got to the motor pool area there were two more vehicles with M60s mounted waiting for us. Morgan assigned a driver and a gunner to each which meant I had to drive one. I was excited: That was the coolest thing I have done in a few days! After a really quick driving lesson which basically came down to: The skinny pedal on the right means Go and the one in the middle means Stop, but never use that one.

Morgan drove one vehicle and he had a gunner. I drove one with a gunner and the other vehicle had a driver and a gunner. I was glad we'd brought four troopers with us. Morgan's vehicle turned out in the lead. They put me in the middle, and the other two troopers fell in the rear.

We started down the feeder of Highway 59 headed north for the beltway. Just like before, the drivers began slowly as they neared the beltway and were taking it easy watching for IEDs as they traveled. Morgan's vehicle slowed and pulled over into the inside lane and the rest of us followed suit. He slowed to a stop and came on the radio and said "Do you see the package lying beside that stalled vehicle ahead of us about forty yards?" We said yes sir. "Stand by. We are shooting and will see if it has an explosive in it." Then the M60 lit up on Morgan's vehicle. The package took a few rounds and then detonated and rocked us all. Morgan said all clear and started driving. I said "So that's it. You say *all clear* and start driving."

He said "Well, I guess I could have said 'Dang, I didn't see that coming.'" I laughed and said to myself *These guys have a sense of humor that only comes from dealing with stuff like this every day. It's like the sense of humor police get after only seeing the dark side of society.* The rest of our drive was uneventful and it gave me time to think about what my first steps would be to get this project going.

I decided once I got a copy of Henson's list of ham operators and their addresses, I would target the ones in the areas I'd said we should cover first: That would be the middle-class neighborhoods to the south of the beltway. I needed to figure out what the message would be and how to keep the groups small so we didn't draw a lot of attention to ourselves. I would start in the neighborhoods south of town and get them to meet in small groups in their neighborhoods at someone's home and not in a public place like a church or convention center. I would coordinate a time to meet them and we would go to the home and discuss the plan and get volunteers. But what to tell them they need to do next?

The first thing was for them to define the perimeter of the subdivision and decide on where they can get coverage to make sure the neighborhood is totally secure. They should also have a few reserves, so in case it got ugly they could call in reinforcements. They would need a failproof system of communications so they could stay in constant contact with each other and call for support as needed. A few might have generators and could keep comms devices charged, but what would those be? Maybe walkie talkies?

We would have to see what resources we could find. Cell towers were only now starting to come back online but were still unreliable, so I would need to find out how many have CB radios, ham operations, or walkie talkies, and see if they can at least get one device per group. If we are lucky enough to have cell service we can use them once everyone gets the numbers in their cells of all the people engaged...

That was it! Portable cell towers! We could ask Henson to request them from cell providers and start putting them in local areas and it would also restrict the service to those in the area. Small cells have a range of one to two kilometers or about a square mile. There are companies that provide those for disaster recovery efforts like in storm areas.

I radioed Morgan and asked him to reach out to Henson and see if we could get portable cell towers to use in the neighborhoods to make sure they had secure communications. He said "Roger that" and switched to Henson's frequency and made the call.

Morgan came back online and said he would see what he could do but he needed to know how many of them we would need. I said "Let's start with ten, and then we will see if we need any more. We will need to have military escort for those things because they could be essential in our efforts."

"Understood."

"If we could cover local neighborhoods with cell service and then reach from group to group with ham operators, we could establish a mesh of communications networks that could cover the entire area and be secure. This could work. Now I just need to see how many guys in Texas will fight."

CHAPTER 13:
OK, BIG MOUTH,
STAND AND DELIVER

We arrived at the base camp Morgan had set up and unloaded with our vehicles in a defensive position. I went to Morgan and said "I have an idea on how we can do this. Want to hear it?"

"Sure. Meet me at my tent in a half hour. I need to get a status update from my team."

In thirty minutes I walked into Morgan's tent and asked if he was ready. He said Yes and asked everyone to excuse him, but asked Kyle to stay. He asked me what I had. I said "I think I have a way to build a mesh of communications networks that will connect our militia together and give us a focused fighting team. First, we need to outfit a truck with a generator and a portable cell tower, then we pull it into the garage of the ham operator in each neighborhood we are trying to set up comms for. Then we'll have cell service for everyone in a local area. We can set it up to work only in a local mode and restrict outbound dialing so we make sure nothing goes in or out that we don't want. The way we do that is to restrict the uplink so it only works locally. We will need some fresh cell phones brought in, just in case the ones in the neighborhoods got fried by the EMP. Besides, that way we keep dedicated phones for security, which is better anyway. We should encourage each family to get with all the families in the neighborhood and share resources. That way we try to keep each family covered.

"We recruit local ex-military guys to find people in the neighborhood who will join the fight and let the recruiting be done locally. But we need to make sure it is positioned as a neighborhood effort to keep everyone protected through food sharing and resource sharing where possible. By doing it locally we reduce the amount of fallout and reduce the risk to our security if they are locally accountable to each other. Our job is to find a local who can lead and they will help set up the perimeter security and decide who can join us in securing the Beltway. Preferably this would be the highest ranking ex-military guy.

"We need to spell out an approach to defense of the neighborhood and that is where I need your help—you can look at the area and define a tactical approach to defense. I will look for someone who does not have their own kingdom in mind but is concerned about the whole group as a leader.

"We will establish a link with the ham operators from our base camp who will then transfer the information to the local leads one day in advance of our coming to get them. We set a time and date to come pick up the recruits they have selected and take them to a secure training facility where Special Forces can train them.

"Our challenge is to get ham operators local to the leads and make sure they are on board with getting the information to them. I would suggest that they have a way to decode it so when the message comes in to the ham operator it doesn't make any sense to him and he will not be able to accidently relay that info to anyone else. All the ham operator needs to know is the message needs to be relayed immediately.

"I also suggest that Henson be ready to arm and equip the recruits we bring to the Special Forces training with military grade equipment if needed. Otherwise they should use their own weapons because they will be familiar with them. The biggest thing will be a show of force and for everyone in the neighborhood to be on watch, with anything unusual to be reported quickly. These creeps are cowards and they will not take you on face to face: They like to hit and run behind a child for cover.

"Should it get really nasty in a neighborhood, we will reserve a trained team to reinforce them if needed. That way the militia is protecting the volunteers and the neighborhood teams and will go in behind you guys to secure the cleared neighborhoods. As we clear them we establish a protection structure and just keep moving until we have the city back.

"The biggest thing I worry about is a vigilante mentality that starts persecuting people in their own neighborhoods. If that happens we just transferred the problem to a different group. So I would recommend as part of our neighborhood support efforts we have either police engaged or someone from the court system so we stay on the path of law and order.

"Oh… and by the way, I would suggest that Henson brief the Governor so he knows what we are doing. I would really hate for him to see us as a group of crazies who have wondered off the reservation. I hope that by now he has determined this is not a police action but an invasion."

Morgan said "Well, you can do that yourself. The Governor already knows about what we are doing and wants a meeting outside of Austin." I asked him when we leave, Morgan said tomorrow morning. He said Henson would be there, along with the two-star responsible for this area.

That evening I spent some time with Morgan just going over things that could happen or possibly go wrong. We ran through at least a hundred scenarios and in each one it fell back on the local groups in the neighborhoods to keep things balanced. After living in several neighborhoods over the years, I wondered if my plan was going to work, because there were some real goofballs in every group. But that is just human nature, I guessed. I reminded myself "It isn't like Star Trek—Mankind is not evolving into a higher life form. You can't fix stupid but you can enforce the law and try to keep everyone safe from an outside threat."

That evening I watched as the fires in the city continued to burn and sometimes seemed to be getting bigger. With no city lights, the fires lit up the horizon and created a surreal picture like the one I had watching the Trade Towers go down. Gunfire was heard frequently in the distance. It reminded me of the scene in *Saving Private Ryan* when the team was walking through Normandy and the flashes and gunfire were seen on the horizon. All of a sudden I felt like I was in a war so I tightened my flak jacket and checked my mags again before lying down under a tree to grab some sleep. Houston was under siege.

At 0400 hours Morgan woke me up and said it was time to roll. I grabbed my pack and laced my boots. I asked Morgan what route he would take to Austin, and he said "I figured we would go back down to Highway 6 and follow it to US 290 and head out west."

"Good idea. The only trouble spot you may have is at Highway 6 and 59 or going through the Stafford area just before it." I pointed to those areas. "Are we meeting Henson at 59 and 6?"

"Yes. They will be there at 0630, so we need to get rolling."

"The most direct route to the Austin area is if we take 6 to 290 and then stay on it all the way to Austin. Hey, Morgan, can we make one stop along the route? It's only two blocks off of 290."

"What for?"

"I need to see if my wife is at my daughter's house. She doesn't know I am alive and I need to check on them. Since they popped the nukes I haven't talked to any of them."

"We can do that."

"And on the way back from Austin we can go down 71 to I-10 and on to highway 6. It's faster and more rural, so we avoid a lot of populated areas."

We turned out on the belt and went south at the I-45 turn to backtrack to highway 6. We had two vehicles and each had a gunner on an M60. One good thing about that time of day was that the trouble makers usually started going in around 0300 or 0400 and the activity was at a low level. The drive down 45 was easy and we all waved as we passed the checkpoint and continued on down to Highway 6. We turned west on 6 and started for Henson's camp.

We reached the Stafford area about 0600 hours and kept on rolling, hoping to avoid any trouble. We almost made it.

Just as we reached the intersection of Highway 6 and Cartwright road, there were a few stalled cars pushed out into the highway. Morgan stopped and pulled out his map to look for a route around the area and we started taking fire from the right-hand side of the road.

Once the shooting started it looked like a scene from the zombie apocalypse. People started running out to shoot at us so we obliged them by returning fire. The two M60's kept the turds pinned down and we made a push through the barricade. There was one spot where two cars were pulled up trunk to trunk so we eased up on them and floored it to push them out of the way and make an opening.

I saw the gunners get at least two as they ran out shooting at the vehicles. They weren't tactically very smart, but I was betting that would change. I was surprised that we didn't find any IEDs. Maybe they were saving those for the beltway. I figured once we made it through the Stafford area things would be easier and they were. We didn't have any more trouble and were getting close to Henson's camp.

Ahead I saw a barricade but it was not stalled cars, it was a checkpoint manned by military. I took a deep breath then and knew we were in a safer spot. As we pulled into Henson's camp, we were greeted by a Lieutenant and directed where to line up with Henson's motorcade. There were six vehicles total, three of them manned by M60 gunners. We pulled out almost immediately. We went north on Highway 6 with no encounters and made it to 290 in about an hour. We turned west on 290 and started toward Hempstead.

A few miles down the road I told the driver where the exit was and how to get to the neighborhood my daughter lived in. Morgan radioed to Henson and said we were making a brief stop and two vehicles were pulling out of the convoy. We would catch back up with them on the east side of Austin. We pulled up in front of the house and I stepped out and started toward the house. Before I could even knock on the door it came open and my daughter was there yelling "Mom, it's Dad!"

Thank the Lord, she had made it! I was so relieved to see that she and the rest of the family were safe. We had a great reunion time and I tried the best I could to explain how I ended up with the National Guard. I compressed eight days into twenty minutes to get through it all.

I really had to get going. There were armed men waiting for me outside. I left instructions for them to try and get back to the bay and gave them the combination to the gun safe. I asked my son-in-law if he could get them there and left him some buckshot for his 12-gauge. If they could get my wife and daughter and the kids to the coast I would feel better because the island was guarded pretty well with only one road in and one road out. I told them to check in with the Tiki PD so they knew they were there. We have a great police force. I asked my wife if she had heard from our son and she said she hadn't yet.

I briefed them all as best I could on what we were trying to do and for my son-in-law to be ready to start talking it up in the neighborhood if things go well with the Governor. I asked him to stay on the island until I had the OK to do the neighborhood watches and then I would get him back to their house unless he was needed on the island for defense. I told my wife I would meet up with her in Galveston as soon as I could get some time to do that but right now I had some commitments I needed to fulfill.

So after hugs and kisses for the grandkids I walked out of the house and headed for the vehicles. When my wife kissed me goodbye at the door I got several cat calls from the troops who were watching, so I made the most out of it and gave her a great big kiss and leaned her way over like you have seen troops do coming home from war. They thought that was great.

Once we pulled back on 290 headed west and crossed the Brazos River we made the turn to Austin. There was a little traffic on the road but not much. I noticed there were no stalled vehicles until we were about thirty miles from Austin. Police were manning a lot of intersections and helping things to move, but the closer we got to Austin, the less traffic we saw. The stalls seemed to have been moved more off to the side of the road and transit was easy. We passed on through on 290 and headed due west to the 71 Highway exit and kept going until the 71 and 290 split just outside of Austin. There we stayed west on 290. I guess we traveled for about another hour before turning on a small farm to market road. Maybe ten minutes down that road there was a barricade manned by Department of Public Safety troops and a few National Guard. After checking our paperwork they waved us through.

We pulled into a ranch house driveway that was the classic ranch house you would expect to see on a large acreage in Texas, except this one had a lot of vehicles and a lot of security. We were instructed on where to park and as we unloaded Henson gave orders for his troops to assist in the security detail and to report to the duty officer on site.

Henson, Morgan and I walked into the front door of the ranch house. We were met by several men who welcomed us and asked us to follow them the Governor was expecting us. We all walked into a large living area and were met by two uniformed military officers, one a two-star, and four men in pressed shirts with no ties. As we engaged in some introductions and casual conversation, Governor Wallace walked in. I had never met the Governor but I did vote for the man. As he walked in it was clear who was in charge in this meeting. So after being invited to sit down I kept my mouth shut and waited to see what would happen next.

Governor Wallace first casually asked everyone how their trip out was, and then asked Henson for a situation report. This was the first time I had heard from Henson his assessment of what was happening and it was stunning. "Governor the National Guard has established a picket line around Houston with the Beltway being our perimeter. We believe for now that the Beltway is secure, but with limited resources if we were to encounter a focused attack we could be overrun. But we do have a little better firepower for now since most of the attacks have been with small arms—however, Governor, our reconnaissance has reported that the areas inside the loop 610 are in trouble. Right now we estimate that between thirty and forty percent of Houston is under radical control. That could mean as many as one million people under siege. Henson pointed to the hot spots and they were from downtown directly north, northeast and southwest of downtown proper. Limited but still noteworthy was the area northwest of downtown. Henson then said "My biggest concern for the immediate future is directly south of downtown. This area is really a hot zone right now." As he went through the areas in turmoil he also began to talk about how organized the fighters were and how the numbers continued to grow each day.

Henson told the Governor how the ISIS implants were stirring up the neighborhoods to get them to riot. They were encouraging looting by telling people "Nobody cares about you, and if you need something you are going to have to take it yourself." In some cases ISIS troops have working vehicles and if the areas close have been looted they are transporting them to loot other areas. In addition, leftists who are wanting a turnover of the country are in a major state of revolt.

"Governor this is like a wildfire or a plague of locusts: As they consume the resources close in, they have to move out to consume more and more, and the perimeter is widening. Power has not been restored in some areas and it is now almost impossible to restore it since crews are taking heavy fire if they try and get in to work on it. We do have power restored in the outlying areas and those areas seem to be targeted more and more as we go through this."

The Governor asked Henson "Are you sure it was organized resistance or is this just unrest from the power and communications being out?"

For the first time I heard Henson say it was clearly organized and it was in fact in his opinion an attempt to overthrow and take control of the entire Houston area. "The tactics are smart. They go into a poor area and get established there. Then when the event occurs they all have a plan on how to organize the community to start the process of assimilation by first encouraging looting. Then ISIS cell leaders begin to lead the neighborhood efforts and they start to expand their control and the footprint of their territory. Their plan is working. I am already hearing that some neighborhoods that are under their control are now being told to convert to Islam or be killed.

"Governor, I am worried about critical assets such as the refineries in the 225 corridor. Oil and Gas production as well as a great deal of shipping coming into the Port of Houston could be at risk very soon. These areas are not only the lifeblood for Houston but for all of Texas and the United States. If workers cannot move to and from work and if we do not provide the proper security for them once on the job we could see not only a shutdown of these functions but we could also see that these critical assets are no longer protected at all."

Governor Wallace looked at Henson and said "Before we go any farther, let me give you an update that I received from a meeting of ten other state Governors I just finished. Texas is alone on this effort inside Texas. Washington DC has basically been taken off the grid and is in total chaos, so we shouldn't count on much help from the US Government at this point. Not that they have been much help lately anyway. So far Mississippi, Louisiana, Georgia and New York are the most heavily engaged and are in worse shape than we are. They did not have the National Guard resources to apply that we have so they are under siege.

"Right now, based on the reports I have, fifty percent of Mississippi appears to be under ISIS control. Georgia has almost totally lost Atlanta. Louisiana has almost lost New Orleans, but they seem to be holding their own for now. Already ISIS has declared Mississippi an Islamic state. They are saying that in New Orleans, but so far they have not been able to take control. The Governor there is pushing back really hard. In Texas we have not lost Houston but it is looking bad. New York has been in a state of police action with a battle line drawn at about 90th street. Harlem is lost to ISIS."

Wallace said "Gentlemen, this is not just a civil uprising or a series of riots, this is a focused attack on the United States and it has been planned for a long time and is starting to work. If they can carve out areas where they have a seat of power inside this country it will just be a matter of time before we are either engaged in a full-out civil war or we are a divided country with states becoming independent Islamic states. Either way, our free America could be over or we will live in a state of war and conflict from now on just like the Middle East.

"This is the most significant event to happen on US soil since the civil war. Even in WWII we did not have the level of conflict here now on our soil as we are seeing today." Once Wallace finished with his update the room was somber.

Governor Wallace looked at Henson and asked "What do you need to first protect what we have and then to begin the task of clearing out areas under ISIS control?"

"First I need troops and equipment. Then we will need a supply line that can keep them functioning. So far we have been effectively using limited resources and have been okay, but if we put in the numbers of assets we need to clean this up, the logistics will become a serious problem. It's the typical wartime scenario: Limited resources means limited impact.

"And right now, we need to shut this thing down before we have an Islamic state on our hands. If we do not find a way to secure the areas we get back they will just fall again so we need a plan going forward. Governor, if you will allow me, I would like to introduce Will Terrell. Mr. Terrell has been working with us as an unofficial consultant since this thing started, and he has some ideas I would like for you to hear. Also, Governor, he is pretty good in a firefight."

Governor Wallace looked at me. "Mr. Terrell what are your ideas?"

Uh-oh, all my big talk and bright ideas were now coming out in a very public forum and I started to doubt my sanity and ability to pull it off. Now that I see the scale of this thing it is big, really big. We are at war with ISIS and Marxism on our own soil.

So I paused for just a moment and then said "Governor Wallace, I believe in the heart of Texas and I do not believe these scum bags are going to win this thing—but having heart is not always enough. We will need a solid strategy and the resource backing to make it happen.

"Governor, thirteen percent of all the US Military comes from Texas. The percentages of people who have served and are able to fight in Texas would be much higher than any other state due to the population. So our plan would be to begin a campaign that targets neighborhoods so far unaffected by the ISIS take over and begin recruiting. I would build a team to go into neighborhoods and begin local meetings to explain what we are doing and look for recruits. We would recruit for two types of people: First would be the local security teams. These teams would stay in the neighborhoods and have 7x24 security watches to prevent the neighborhood from being overrun and to prevent disorder. We would want this team to work in cooperation with local law enforcement and be under law enforcement supervision. We would train the local neighborhood security teams on what to look for and how to maintain a safe approach to security. In addition we would teach the neighborhoods about how to work together to support the entire neighborhoods with food and water as well as keeping up the neighborhood watch. We do not want vigilantes, and that is why all security efforts are monitored by law enforcement. I will come back to resources we will need for this group in a moment.

"The second group recruited would be former military, and preferably those with some combat experience as well as logistics and communications, to begin the active security force effort. Once Henson's team clears and secures an area the second civilian or militia team will move in and secure the locations and make sure they stay protected. I would request that Special Forces be sent in to conduct training efforts for this team. If they have trained the terrorists to fight they can train us. After all most all of the Afghans were trained to fight the Russians by our own special forces.

"This training team will need more logistical support since they will be away from their local neighborhood and dependent upon us supporting them. These teams will be under direct orders from Henson and his team and will fall under military guidelines for engagement and behavior. Once Henson moves in and takes an area, the second team secures it and maintains going forward so Henson's team can move to the next area.

"My greatest fear is the terrorists have learned how to hide behind women and children. They will go back in their houses and look totally innocent and then shoot us in the back. If we do not leave security teams they will just start all over again. Soft targets become more vulnerable once the military moves on.

"I am worried about how we find them all and remove them. Hiding is their strong suit, so we will need a high level of cooperation from the neighborhoods to find and remove the problems. This can be scary: We do not want this to turn into a holocaust, but we will need to know who has been involved with the ISIS fighters. So we will rely only partially on word of mouth but we will need an intelligence group who can filter information. That should come from the military and not the militia.

"Another question we must have answered very clearly is what to do with them after they are found, and what the rules of engagement are. I am hoping that once an area is clear and the security forces move in, we can begin the building of neighborhood teams right away so they can secure and police themselves internally. We may need a large detainment area that we can put prisoners of war. We did it during WWII and we may want to think about it again. But this time we need to have better vetting so we do not imprison non-offenders.

"Now, let me address some resources we will need for both groups, but mostly for the neighborhood security teams. We will need generators and small cell sites for each neighborhood. A small cell site will cover about a square mile and will provide a local communications link that will be restricted to the phones we would provide.

"A set of cell phones that would be turned up for the cell site would be great since we could secure them and only those phones could get on the network. Without an uplink to the wider net the network would be secure and localized. We can control who gets the uplinks and we would have leaders in the area that would be in communications with a command post established for neighborhood support in the area. Preferably the leaders will be ex-military.

"In the command post we would need rapid response teams who could roll on a security issue if needed, and it would be best if they were from the second team who would have military experience.

"It may become necessary to provide food and water relief to some of these neighborhoods if we cannot get power back on soon. But I am hooping with the security teams in place our crews can work those issues much faster.

"I would expect that the neighborhood security teams could provide their own weapons. If they do not have them then we would put them in a higher support type of role. If they do not have their own weapons I am not comfortable with them carrying one. If it gets ugly to the point that they need more ammo then we should already have the support teams there carrying the fight.

"If our objective is to move and secure and then move and secure more areas we will run out of troops really fast if we do not leave a team behind that is local and will stay there. This will look more like an occupational effort than a police effort. In some ways that is true so they may need resources and supplies, and part of our supply chain effort must be armed escort for supplies. If we do this right, we start to starve out ISIS and they will be desperate for supplies, then our supply lines become targets. Then we start to take them out as they try to intercept. In addition the more desperate they become the more out in the open they will start to move."

I looked at Governor Wallace. "Well those are the basics of my plan, sir. However, I do have one thing that haunts me. While we are trying to retake our homes, who is closing the borders so we do not fight a never-ending trail of terrorists coming in? After all, that is how most of them got here in the first place. Nothing personal, Governor, but we cannot afford for the US Government to use this as an opportunity to declare martial law, and we have all seen how competent they are at running the country, so for them to take responsibility and to say they will manage it would mean a disaster of biblical proportions. Not to mention that if we do have the citizens engaged because there is no way the military and the police can handle this thing, the US will declare martial law and before you know it we'll have a police state."

Wallace looked at Henson and paused for a beat or two and said "Mr. Terrell, if you can get this done I will focus on the border and what we do with any hostiles once captured. We will keep them off your back and prevent reinforcements. When can you start?"

"I already have, sir." Wallace told Henson "Talk with the two-star and get whatever he needs to take back Houston." He stood up and shook my hand and said "Good luck and Godspeed to you, Mr. Terrell. The fate of Texas may be in your hands." He smiled.

"No pressure."

CHAPTER 14:
EATING THE ELEPHANT
ONE BITE AT A TIME

We loaded up in the vehicles to get started back and Henson looked at me and said "Are you ready for this?"

"Whether I'm ready or not, it looks like it has to happen, and whether we wanted a war or not, it is here."

On the ride back, Henson, Morgan, and I talked about how we would stage supplies coming in and where the areas should be as well as how the supply lines would be protected. Next we discussed the protection of the 225 corridor for the refineries and how we needed a plan for them right away.

Driving back, Morgan and I discussed the neighborhoods in the area and where we should recruit first. We discussed how many we would need both at a minimum and what to do if we had extras. Next we discussed how to conduct training, and Henson said our Special Forces guys knew how to do that, and it could be neighborhood focused. My hope was that Texas would stand and deliver with not only soldiers but would show the rest of the world what makes up our heart. This is our generation's Alamo moment.

Five hours of discussion and strategy made the trip back seem shorter. We pulled into Henson's camp about 2100 hours, and could see the skyline lit up by fires from about eight miles away. It was getting worse in Houston. As soon as we pulled in, Henson asked for a situation report from the Lieutenant, asking me to sit in.

Lieutenant Daniels started with the situation of his troops. He had only one casualty who was not critical but was in the hospital. He said "All the reports coming back are saying that it looks like the neighborhood south of downtown and the one northeast of downtown have been totally taken over by radicals. We're seeing some people leaving the neighborhoods, but many are trapped and have no way to get out if they wanted to.

"Most of the businesses in those areas had been looted and were now on fire. The Fire Department cannot go in because of the heavy fire they take so they are watching it burn. Some of the areas close by these neighborhoods have already started to see some looting. Since food and water resources are running out in the worst areas they are expanding their footprint to take in more resources. Moving into those areas was easier for them than we thought it would be since many areas cleared out worrying about their family's safety.

"A fairly affluent area around Rice University is under siege now. The stores are being looted and some homes are being burned. The insurgents are now getting better and more proactive with IEDs. Seems our scout teams are finding them regularly on the loop and occasionally on the beltway. Most major highways into and out of the city are blocked with stalled cars, most of them burned-out wrecks. We have no estimate of dead or wounded in the city but our teams report having seen corpses on the roadways. Most likely people trying to get out or were killed trying to protect their property. We have no estimate of what it is like in the neighborhoods themselves.

"We have on three different occasions intercepted trucks carrying weapons and ammo into the city. They have probably figured out alternate routes by now so we don't have any idea how much they're being supported. Our problem is we don't have enough manpower to cover every possible route into a city this size. We need air surveillance and we need the authority to shoot if we suspect weapons traffic. But the problem is that inside the city it will be hard to target weapons movement without some collateral damage to civilians. We are looking at ways to monitor outside the city in the more rural areas and be more preemptive in our approach."

"Would it be possible to establish a circle of death? Meaning that if anything looking suspicious within a certain area, we could take it out."

"That is only in a declaration of war. We're not there yet."

"We now have three drones rotating in and out of coverage but there's too much real estate for only three. We need at least three or four more just to have a presence. The Houston-Woodlands-Sugar Land metropolitan area has a total area of 10,062 square miles. 8,929 square miles of that is land area, while 1,133 square miles is water area. It's only slightly smaller than Massachusetts and slightly larger than New Jersey. I have no idea how many roads can be used to get into the city but there are probably several hundred."

I asked "Do we have access to the road cameras around Houston, since they are on all the major roads? That could ease the burden some for watching the major roads and then let the drones do more rural coverage." Henson approved the idea and instructed Lt. Daniels to get with the city and see how we could tap into the camera feeds. Henson also asked for Lt. Daniels to find a secure office building where we could set up a better command post and to make sure we have wideband and radio communications established.

After the debrief, Henson said "Morgan you need to set a battle plan, and Terrell you need to set a recruiting plan. Together you need to set a plan for security after the battle. You two get that worked out and I need to see it in forty-eight hours. Things are escalating and we need to get moving on shutting this down. Your rules of engagement are, if you're shot at, shoot back with extreme prejudice. If you get a prisoner you think we get some intel from, bring them in. I will assign an Intel officer to your team. What else will you need?"

Morgan said "We need timelines for generator arrivals and small cell sites. We'll need technicians who can install the small cell sites for us. We'd like to have them preconfigured before we roll them out to the neighborhoods."

"OK. What else?"

"We need to know when Special Forces arrive so we can take them with us when we start recruiting. They may have some good insight into that process."

"Agreed, but you will be building a battle plan. Terrell has to do the recruiting." I felt a pucker go over all my body, and I am pretty sure I left a pucker mark on my chair, too. All of a sudden it hit home what was happening and how much responsibility I had, and this was no small deal.

Henson asked "Is there anything else?" Morgan and I looked at each other and shook our heads *No*. "Well, then, gentlemen. we all have work to do, so let's get busy."

Morgan and I walked out of Henson's tent. We looked at each other and at the same time said "Holy crap." Just as we started to move toward our vehicle a soldier walked up to us and asked if we were Morgan and Terrell. We said yes and he introduced himself as Lou Torez with the Army Special Forces. I said "Wow, you guys are fast! We just asked when you would be here."

"Swift and precise response is what we do, sir." We both shook his hand and said it was a pleasure to meet him. Morgan told Torez "Your job is to protect Terrell and to give guidance on neighborhood recruitment and training."

Torez looked a little puzzled but he turned to me and said "When do we start?"

"How about now? Grab your gear. We are going on a field trip and it may involve a lot of door-to-door selling. We leave here at 0400 for Morgan's base camp."

Torez went to find a place to grab a nap and we went to find some food and then went into a visiting officer's tent to find bunks to crash on for the next four hours. At 0400 Morgan rousted me, and we gathered up our gear and started walking to the vehicles. Torez walked up with his pack and weapon and didn't say a word. I looked at Morgan and smiled and said "I like this guy already." All three of us walked to Morgan's vehicles and climbed in: Morgan in the first vehicle with a gunner and two support troops, with Torez and me in the second with a driver. The third was manned with a gunner and a driver.

As we pulled out I noticed that Torez never took his eyes off of the surroundings. He looked at everything, and his threat detector was amazing, yet he could still carry on a conversation as long as it wasn't too intense. so I asked him if he had a family. "Yes sir: a wife and a son three years old."

I asked him where they lived and he said outside of San Antonio. I asked him if he has talked to them since all of this went down and he said "Yes. Things are okay, but they were scared. My wife's family lives there so she has support locally. Do you have a family?"

"Yes. At least I hope I still do. My wife was at my daughter's house. I am not sure about my son and his family." I told Torez about my walkathon and meeting Morgan and the development of our plan.

He sat there quietly and kept scanning, and then he turned and looked at me and said "This plan can work sir. I have lived in Texas all of my life and if there is a bunch of people who will fight it is Texans."

I nodded. "I sure hope so. It may be the only way we can save the country."

With no surprises, we rolled up on Stafford and guess what? The car blockade was back, only this time it was bigger and more solid, so we pulled up a GPS and found a route through the neighborhood that would skirt the barricade. Torez checked his mag, so I did too. The gunners both locked and loaded the 60s, and we made a sudden turn right and started blasting through the neighborhood.

We only needed to go four blocks to get around the blockade. Once we turned we saw several turds run from the blockade toward the neighborhood so we figured there would be a fight but we hoped it would happen so fast they wouldn't be able to react very much.

It almost worked: Three cut us off at the entrance back onto the highway and started firing on our vehicles with small arms that had little effect on armor but our reaction was a little more devastating.

All three were cut down in about two seconds. we made the turn and were rolling again. No cars chased us at first, and then a small pickup turned out on the highway and started coming after us. We had armor but were not very fast, so he was closing the gap quickly. Morgan told the gunner in the last vehicle "Wait until this vehicle's a hundred yards from us, and if they keep chasing us, take them out."

At one hundred yards the gunner opened up and the truck was hit all throughout the grill and windshield. It swerved and then exploded in a massive fireball. The gunner came on the radio and told Morgan it was rigged to blow with what looked like propane or gasoline. It lit up all the area for a couple hundred yards around it while it burned. We kept rolling as fast as we could go.

We returned the same way we came, via Highway 6 to I-45 and then turned north. I heard Morgan on the radio tell Kyle we were coming in from the south. We rolled up on Kyle's blockade and checked in to see how they were doing.

He said it had been fairly routine since we left and there hadn't been any more fire exchanges. We waved and said we were rolling back to Morgan's camp and started out. Like last time, we turned back over to Highway 3 and went in the back way and tried to stay off of I-45 and the more crowded areas. We pulled into Morgan's camp around 1100 hours, grabbed a couple of MREs and went inside Morgan's tent.

We laid out a big map of Houston and started determining which areas we should focus on first. We decided that the neighborhoods right around the 225 corridor would be best since many of those people probably worked at the refineries and we knew they were mostly hard hat neighborhoods full of blue collar guys who would be willing to fight.

We listed the neighborhoods by priority and ease of transition when moving from one to another, discussed how Morgan would clear the refinery areas and then we would follow up with security. I needed about two or three weeks to make sure I had the right people and Torez had a chance to do some training. Hopefully we would find a lot of ex-military and the training would be minor.

We documented our strategy and put it into phases:

Phase 1

- *Meet with local law enforcement to inform them of what we are doing and establish a working relationship with them.*

- *Engage a coordinated effort with private security groups who work the refinery and ship channel area.*

- *Recruit in the Pasadena/Deer Park area.*

- *Establish training times and locations and determine how many can stay on neighborhood watch and how many can join us guarding the refineries.*

- *Cover all immediate area neighborhoods with same approach.*

- *Call in the small cell and generator units and set them up with an established communications protocol. Based on our calculations we would need three small cell sites for this area alone.*

Phase 2

- *Relieve Morgan's team at the 225 refineries and move to the next critical area.*

- *That area would be the neighborhoods more north and east of the refineries on the beltway.*

- *The same approach as phase 1 would be needed because the ship channel would be along that route and more refineries.*

- *This will be another extremely critical set of assets to cover.*

- *Set up neighborhood watches and recruit troops to relieve Morgan.*

- *This area we determined may need five small cell sites. But the refineries had generators so power would not be as big an issue.*

Phase3

- *Have a response team trained and ready to roll to either the refinery row on 225 or the ship channel.*

- *This team may need to be at least 20 strong with military hardware to respond in this large an area.*

- *From our recruits we will try to find seasoned battle veterans who were recently in combat situations.*

The remaining phases would be done based on geography and demographics to determine which areas we are most likely to get recruits from. Our focus would be to get as many recruits as possible as quickly as possible, so when we go into other neighborhoods we can go with a presence that shows force and structure. Torez will be training trainers as well, so we can divide and train more recruits.

Morgan's plan read like a suburban guerilla warfare guideline. He would first deploy his forces in strategic locations and prepare them for a *Roll!* command that would send them into the areas we are clearing. Each group would be supported by armor and there would be no less than a platoon in each staging area. There were plenty of details and after reading them I felt comfortable. Morgan would clear the road then I would need to come in behind him and plow it.

Morgan fed our battle plans into the computer and sent them to Henson, and then we waited for his response, so for the next five hours we rested up. I took a little nap and ate some more MREs.

Then Morgan came out of his tent and said "Terrel, I just heard from Henson. He said the Governor approved the plan and to get started immediately."

I found Torez and acquired a vehicle with a gunner and a driver and we targeted the first neighborhood. Morgan began to prepare his troops for their move to the refineries. I heard Morgan radio Kyle and have him move his team up to the beltway and 45 with the barricade and place it on the beltway just north of 45, which would leave the local police manning the barricade where they were at that time.

Morgan handed me a contact name and number with addresses on it for the local police departments in Pasadena and Deer Park. "The Governor notified them all of them what we were doing, but said it would be a good idea to go visit them to reduce any confusion or hurt feelings. Could you go visit them and notify them what we're doing and stand by to assist if needed? It's mostly so they don't get upset that we are coming onto their turf. Just explain the plan we have and tell them that they will be in charge of local law enforcement representation in the neighborhoods, while we help recruit and train people. The locals will be in charge after we leave."

Lopez looked different in battle gear, and it was impressive. He handed me a vest that covered down to my crotch and a Kevlar helmet. He asked if I had a side arm and I showed him my .45. He checked my weapon and then he checked my M4 and spare mags. It made me feel better about going into a situation like this with him on my side. I asked him if he thought I might need some bug repellent he said "Don't worry, I have that," and lifted his M4.

We climbed into our vehicle. I gave the driver directions on where we were headed and sat in the back seat. Lopez sat in the shotgun seat. Our gunner was riding up on the mount with his wraparound sunglasses on to block the wind. We started out. The first neighborhood we came to was a very middle class housing area that looked like it ranged in price between $150k and $300k. It was so close to the storage tanks at Ellington I was sure if those tanks took a hit this neighborhood would go up in a flash. We pulled in and stopped at the first house on the right.

We got out slowly and carefully. I left my M4 in the vehicle but Lopez had his slung, and we approached the front door. The driver and our gunner stayed in the vehicle. I asked the gunner to not stand at the weapon. I rang the doorbell and when a female voice came from behind the door asking who was there, I answered "US Army, ma'am. May we have a word with you and your husband, please?" She said her husband was not there and she was not comfortable opening the door. I told her I understood and asked if it would be OK if we came back later. She said it would, and we turned to leave, but just then the door opened and a young woman in her early forties opened the door and said "Can I help you?"

We turned around and removed our head gear and made sure we were staying a safe distance away so she would not feel threatened. I began by asking her what she knew about the problems we were having in Houston and some surrounding areas. She replied "Yes, I have heard some things."

I told her we were a group of National Guard that had been sanctioned by the Governor to build local neighborhood watch teams and we were just starting to canvass her neighborhood. As she listened intently, she slowly stepped out of her front door and stood with her arms crossed while I went through our plan for her neighborhood and how we were setting up a security group to protect her and her family.

Her first question was "Do you know when we will have power fully restored?"

I said "Actually, making the neighborhoods safe for power teams to come in is part of the reason we're doing this." She uncrossed her arms, which to me said she was feeling more secure, and said "Would you men like to come inside?"

I said "Yes, ma'am, but we can't stay very long. We have a lot of ground to cover." Torez and I walked in the house behind her. She asked us to have a seat. The house was modest, but you could tell there was pride in what she had, and it felt like a home to me.

She introduced herself and asked if we would like some iced tea or water, I said "Iced tea sounds really good. We don't get much iced tea with our MREs."

Lopez grinned and said "Yes, ma'am, that sounds great." She disappeared for four or five minutes and came back with two glasses of tea. It was obvious this woman was accustomed to southern Texas style hospitality.

She said "OK, so you guys are building a group to provide security for our neighborhood."

"Yes, ma'am, and yours will not be the only one. We will continue to move all the way through Texas if we have to so we can eliminate these turds. ...Oops! Sorry, ma'am, I mean these *insurgents*."

She laughed and said "I have called them much worse. No offense taken."

I asked her if her husband was at work and she said yes, and that he worked at a refinery on 225. I asked if they had any children and she said two, both at school and she'd be walking to the school to meet them in a couple of hours.

"Have you seen any issues with security or have there been any strangers in the neighborhood lately?"

"N-no, but my husband has seen some observers around his plant and it made him really nervous. The plants had their own source of power, so they've been functioning while most of the neighborhoods around here have had intermittent power for the past couple of weeks."

"Has your husband got a military background?"

"Yes! Army. Got out six years ago and went to work for a refinery right away. We have been married for eight years. I was an Army wife for two years, and we had our first child in the housing at Fort Hood. Our second was born just after he got out and took the job here."

I asked her what her husband did in the Army and she said he was a Staff Sergeant working supply and logistics. I made a note: This was handy to know! I asked her if he ever saw combat and she said "Not really. He was in Afghanistan and Iraq, but his job was keeping the forces supplied with what they needed. He didn't spend much time on the front lines."

We thanked her and said "We need to get moving but we would really like to meet your husband because we won't be successful in what we're trying to do if we can't depend on guys like him who've moved resources around to keep an Army going. When he gets in would you please tell him we will stop by later? What time does he get home?"

She said "5:30 PM." I checked my watch. That was about four hours away. I thanked her again and started for the door with Lopez. She said "I have just one question."

"Yes, ma'am, what would that be?"

"Will you kill these scum bags trying to destroy our country?"

I looked at Lopez and said "Ma'am, that is our intent."

"Well, kill all of them."

I nodded and stepped out of the front door. We turned to our right and went on to the next house in line and knocked. No one was home so I left a note on the door saying we would have a neighborhood meeting in two days and we would appreciate their attendance. I signed it Colonel Terrell, Texas militia. I'd just made myself a Colonel! I figured in Texas that carried some weight so why not?

I guessed I had better tell Morgan so he wouldn't think I was crazy with an ego that was going out of control. Lopez shook his head and said "You know, you might have been pretty good in the head game aspect in Afghanistan. I could have used you."

I grinned and said "Look, buddy, I have been in the IT business for 40 years. I know head games."

He grinned. "OK, next house."

As we continued down through the neighborhood, our vehicle escort flanked us all the way. We had roughly a twenty percent success rate at finding people home. Most were housewives. A couple were men who worked night or evening shifts at the plants, but by and large it had been a strikeout, in my opinion. We hoped that by putting a note on their door calling for a neighborhood meeting we would get some responses, so we would have a representation of the neighborhood and we could meet more men, which was what we wanted.

So we canvassed the neighborhood and left hand-written notes on every door or handed them to whoever was home after our little speech, which had now been refined, and we pulled out of the neighborhood. I wasn't sure if we made progress or not, and I was starting to doubt my grand idea was attainable. We decided that since it was still early we would stop by the house we first talked with and see if the husband was home.

There was a new car in the driveway... or should I say a Ford F-150. That is what I am talking about, a true Texas limousine. I liked this guy already. We stopped and walked up to the door and before we could even knock the door opened. A guy about six foot and fit opened the door and said "Yes, sir, may I help you?"

"Well, sir, I think the helping thing could be mutual. Do you have a few minutes to talk?"

"I do. Please come in."

After introductions we again sat in the living room of this comfortable and non-threatening home and discussed what we were attempting to do. The man listened quietly and very intently and once we were done he simply asked "How can I help?"

That was all we needed to hear, so we spelled out what we needed from a logistical support standpoint in the neighborhood and how we would start right here and then move our boundaries out as we could. He said "I'm in. What's next?"

"Talk to all the neighbors you can and have them at the meeting in two days where we can present the plan to all of your neighbors."

"I will do that."

We got up to leave. Before we walked out, he said "You know, when I was in the Army, I never pulled a single trigger at an enemy combatant, but now with my home possibly under attack I can do that and would not hesitate."

I looked at the young man and said "Sir, before this went down, I had never pulled a trigger at an enemy either. But war changes things, and war at home changes everything."

CHAPTER 15:
RESERVATIONS TO THE DANCE

After visiting our first neighborhood we had found ten men who would be willing to act as neighborhood guards with another possible twelve if they worked out. Only about half had previous military experience, but it was more than we had. In each case they had either served in the military in years past or were hunters who had weapons. Not bad for a first pass.

Going into the second neighborhood, we had a much more refined script and knew what buttons to push. We expected each one to be easier from our standpoint as far as how the message was being sent but we expected the results to vary based on the demographics of each neighborhood.

I scheduled for Torez to meet the first group with me at the home of one of the volunteers in two nights. That gave us some time to build the training exercises we wanted, and I could cover two more neighborhoods in the meantime.

The next day we went to the adjoining neighborhood on our list to visit. It was better as far as interest and commitment from the residents.

I scheduled a meeting with Torez and me in three days to train them. This group produced thirteen volunteers for neighborhood security, and we got three recently in the military who would join our team of outside security militia. There were still another nine who we would follow up with who could rotate in and out of security operations.

After the third neighborhood, we had enough volunteer security to cover all three neighborhoods, and we had a total of seven recent military staffers who we would use in outside security. Seven was good but it was not enough to really cover the critical assets.

The third night, when we went back into the first neighborhood to train, we were amazed at how many men—and some women—were there. The invitations to the local law enforcement had been accepted and we had a great turnout representing the police. I had allowed them a thirty-minute time slot to discuss law and how their roles would be utilized in this effort. They were great.

The numbers were at least double what we had figured would be there. The individuals we had talked with had been recruiting in the neighborhood on their own, and had grown the base significantly. In the classic Texas hospitality sense, we had ladies bring in drinks and whatever snacks could be gathered and I was amazed at how much good stuff was there considering most of it was prepared on gas grills or in BBQ pits. We were also able to add two more outside security members.

The next night it was more of the same, and so was the third night. Now we had fifteen outside security team members and at least fifteen to twenty for each neighborhood for security. *This could work after all*, I thought. I went to each of the outside security team members and gave them a couple of days to get their things in order, and to buy Torez and me a couple of days to get a solid training plan in place.

I think what amazed me in the meetings was how mad and determined these teams were. Protecting their homes was a basic instinct, but what I was most amazed at was the fifteen who said we will fight to cover the country's critical assets. That made me proud to be a Texan.

Torez was amazing as he showed each group how to build a schedule for who was covering and the areas they would cover. He also had a plan for how each person had an alternate in the event they were sick. He inspected their weapons and positioned them to guard the neighborhoods based on the weapons they had. His basic approach was to put rifles in some areas to cover more ground, shotguns in other areas for closer action but needing more effect, and handguns only if it got bad.

We coordinated the arrival of the generators and small cell towers. Phones were handed out, and instructions on charging them were included so that the repository for phone chargers was at the generator and the generator itself had an armed guard.

The first three sites were up. It only took us six days to get them online. I reported back to Henson what our success rate had been and he was amazed. I could tell it really surprised him we had been that successful. He asked if we could use another Special Forces guy and could we move faster if we had one. I said "Yes but I can't divide and conquer like that so I'll need to train someone to assist and do what I have been doing. Can you recommend me a wing man?"

"I'll work on that and let you know."

Next day, Kyle was on the team. That was great: Now we could start to spread out and cover more ground. My first objective was to have Kyle go with me to the next neighborhood and see how we talked with the people and how we got things set up. He was a natural at communicating and being an instructor on how we'd do things. I should have known he would be, after all, he'd spent his days teaching kids how to stay alive under the worst possible scenarios.

Now it felt like we were rolling. We had covered four neighborhoods and had recruited security teams in each one, as well as found forty ex-military for the team. Lopez had asked for and received three more Special Forces guys to assist in the training. Momentum was building. It was just in time.

After attending the fourth neighborhood recruiting meeting it was evident that word had been passed to ISIS on what we were doing. Just as we pulled out of the neighborhood, we got lit up. We had small arms fire coming in from all around us. The M60 started returning fire and all five of us in the truck rolled out to find cover.

One was hit as soon as he stepped out, but luckily it struck his vest so he was not badly hurt. We drug him in behind the vehicles and started returning fire with extreme prejudice. I saw a couple of turds take hits and go down from the 60 and at least two more from our guys returning fire. Our guys could shoot: the others, not so much. They kept us pinned down but they seemed a lot more worried about staying in cover than they were at actually trying to hit a target.

We had been engaged about five minutes when I noticed that fire started coming from a little behind us and to the sides. The neighborhood team had already started making their presence known. That was awesome. One of the locals with a deer rifle nailed a guy who had been keeping the guys in the first vehicle hunkered down since they stopped. The insurgent had an automatic weapon that sounded like an AK and was putting some serious lead down range, but a well-placed round from a .30 caliber deer rifle ended all of that. Once he went down, the others seemed to lose some interest and started pulling back. A couple of them didn't make it. As they turned to leave, they became targets and our guys nailed them.

Once the turds cleared out, we had the security team go ahead and set up shop and start their watch. They had not had all the training we wanted to give them but we could not afford for the turds to come back and make an example out of the neighborhood for working with us.

Lopez quickly looked at a map of the neighborhood and deployed the fire teams for maximum coverage. After they were in place and within eyesight of each other—since we didn't have all the comms in yet—we felt better about leaving, so we rolled out.

I told Lopez that the game had just changed and now they were on to us, so we would need to be more vigilant in how we approached the neighborhoods and would need to be ready to fight as soon as we pulled out. That scared me a little, but at the end of the day they would have to fight whether we were there or not, so they might as well get started.

The reality was that once we told the other neighborhoods what was happening and that turds were watching all the neighborhoods and would get to them eventually the number of volunteers started to go up even more. But I also realized that now there could be informants in almost every neighborhood. This could get a lot worse than I thought.

I started wondering what happens once the neighborhoods find out and start their own brand of informant removal. Everything we worked for to get a balance and justice focused on the law could be thrown out for frontier justice. We could be creating a monster. We couldn't ask the police to do the monitoring because now we'd have a police state. That sounded like Nazi Germany. So what is the solution?

I went back to how our country was founded. It was built to mirror how the Israelites were structured by Moses under God's direction to have local judges. They handled the small stuff, but all local matters had to have a foundation of the Ten Commandments as a base. I determined that local communities needed to establish their own guidelines, but they needed to have a foundation of basic law and know that our laws were where they drew the line. The law must be followed, but local management of the problems was the best solution.

Community judges needed to be established, and they had to be done by the police and justice system.

This hadn't been done in America since the early 1900s. Could it be accomplished again? We have been told we needed to evolve, we needed to progress beyond where we were as a country. In reality, what we have been taught is we need to be weak so that others may be strong. Most of humanity takes the approach "We must make them weak so we will look strong."

In my view a return to local involvement and a stable justice system was our only hope if we were going to get back the Great American experiment and become what we have been and could be again.

I had Torez turn around and head back to the first neighborhood we had been in. I met with the leadership team and told them what they needed to do—appoint a local neighborhood representative to act as a judge on local issues—but they were not to hand out punishment if problems were found. If someone was found to be treasonous and telling our enemy what is going on, they needed to call the local police, also any other issues breaking the laws of the land were to be reported to the police. We repeated this message at each of the neighborhoods we had been in previously.

Now we had a good plan. We told the entire story, including the local judge efforts, at each new neighborhood we went into. It felt natural, and people responded very positively.

Just as I was starting to think we would be able to get this done we had a bad turn. We received a radio message from Henson telling us that we were needed back at Morgan's base as soon as we could get there. We had just finished up with our updates to all the neighborhoods we had covered so the timing was good. We had only secured eight neighborhoods, but it was enough that we had security in each of them and had a force of about fifty being trained to help guard critical assets along the ship channel and refinery row. Our geographical coverage was only about five miles along the beltway around the ship channel. There was a lot more area we needed to cover to be truly effective and not leave any holes in our security.

We rolled back into Morgan's camp area and were met by a soldier who asked us to come with him. In Morgan's tent, he didn't even say hello before he started telling us about a problem they were having. I figured it must be bad. Morgan said "Inside the loop, Houston is basically a loss. The police have pulled back to the beltway and we are just watching the city burn. We have to accelerate our timeline of going into the city to clear out the enemy as soon as possible."

"Where do you want to start?"

"That's why you're here. I need some local knowledge to build a plan and I need a plan now."

"OK. What do you need?"

"How many recruits were you able to get that can do outside work?"

"Just about fifty, and they're being trained now." I told him what we had set up in each of the eight neighborhoods we had been in so far. He asked point blank if I thought this would work.

"Well, it was how we built this country, and it's how God instructed the Israelites to build theirs, so I have to assume it will work. It has worked for a few thousand years so far."

"OK. Let's see if we can take back Houston. Terrel, If you can help me build a plan and we can use the fifty you have so far, I'll get started and you can keep building our forces. Once you've completed all of the neighborhoods we've targeted, you can rejoin our forces and we will get this thing done. "

He showed me where we had forces positioned and gave me basic troop counts. They were positioned in a star-shaped five location structure surrounding the city. I pointed out the areas I felt would be the heaviest resistance and suggested we should go there last for two reasons: one, we could reclaim a lot of territory without a great deal of loss, and two, that it would also buy me time to strengthen our resources so we had more troops to take the tough areas. Morgan also said his key objectives would be to take back the business and commercial areas first because he felt the enemy headcount would be lower and spread out more. In theory that sounded right but if the resources had been exhausted in the neighborhoods they would be reaching out to other areas to feed the machine. But by doing that they would have to provide a logistical way of moving people and spoils back to the hoods. That could be a weakness.

Morgan said, "I think it should begin with Special Forces recon teams checking out the areas and coming back with on-the-ground intelligence. I'd start with the Galleria area first."

"Do you have troop coverage? And do the areas close by have a heavy enemy troop count?"

"Yes, and in fact I'm sort of hoping this will draw them to the area as a diversion so we can retake the other areas faster. In my opinion these punks have limited resources and limited trained fighters—mostly a bunch of thugs carrying guns. So if I can draw the best troops into a conflict in one area I could use that to put an effort on the other areas and make more progress."

"What type of support would you have for your team in that area? Because you probably shouldn't underestimate how many fighters they will have."

"I'll have air support and armor, but I'm going to wait until they're fully engaged to use it so we can trap as many as possible in the kill zone. In my estimation, the vast majority of the enemy fighters will be coming from the southwest and the west. I'd put my heaviest troop counts supporting those areas but have air support for backup in the other areas. In some very select cases I could use artillery since the smart ammo used in them today is so accurate."

I pointed out some strategic buildings with great views that would allow his spotters and snipers to have a large field of fire. I told him about the underground areas around the mall and how these could be used to transport personnel unseen. I suggested a few critical areas that they may try to come in from and then watched as he put together the first effort to retake Houston. He was very good at building a strategy and I hoped that everything I had heard about the fog of war was not true and we could pull this off.

CHAPTER 16:
ITS GO TIME

Morgan asked me to accelerate the training for the fifty troops we had and to get them to him as fast as possible. I told him I would need transportation, and he would need to get them equipment so they would be ready. He said he would send choppers to get them when we were ready and not to worry about the logistics: He had that covered.

I asked him where he wanted me now and he said for me to get back to my neighborhoods and keep building an army for him. I said "I can do that," and Lopez and I started back to our vehicle.

But as I was walking, I thought of something else and went back into Morgan's tent. I asked "Is there any way you could get us more Special Forces so they could take on additional neighborhoods and we would be able to cover a lot more than we are doing now?"

"I'll work on that and let you know."

Our escort vehicle included Lopez, our driver, a gunner, and myself. We loaded up and started back to cover our neighborhoods. Now I had an increased sense of urgency to get as many resources for these efforts as I could. I felt like we were losing Houston, and we could lose Texas. We must not let that happen.

Driving back, I started thinking about my wife, my daughter's family, my son, and his family, and I began to really feel the pressure of how this event was turning into a full-scale war. I had the resources of an army with me, but my family was on their own. I just couldn't lose any of them so I had to do what I could to make sure that didn't happen.

Then it hit me that I had not talked to my son since this thing started. What was his status? Were they OK? These issues started to make me shrink back and reflect. Had I told him enough about possible scenarios and how would he react to them? Did I do my job as a parent to make sure he would have a plan and they would be all right?

All of this started to build on me and I started to feel like there was more I should have done. I know it was the country at stake, but I still had a family to protect. After all, they were who I was fighting for, and for families just like them all across the country.

Then I realized that my plan could be expanded to include their areas first. Each of them had connections and resources that could be valuable, including some former snipers and military that each of them knew. They could really help get the neighborhoods secured and help us build some invaluable additional resources.

I started building a recruiting plan that would target their neighborhoods, where I knew I could get some additional resources.

Once we arrived back at camp, I started a fast assessment of the areas where we needed to do the neighborhood recruiting. As it turned out, the areas were perfect for possible resources, as they were mostly middle-class neighborhoods and many of the people there had been in the military before.

My first stop was to my son's neighborhood. It was great to see they were all fine, and as I had suspected, he had several of his friends already working on the security of the neighborhood. Once we started the recruitment efforts, it was even better than I had hoped. We got an additional fifteen fighters and a solid security team to cover the area.

I asked my son to cover the security detail in the neighborhood since he did not have military experience—however he had several friends who did, and a couple of them had been snipers so they knew how to fight and knew good, solid tactics.

Morgan was really excited that we brought fifteen back with us to assist in the retaking of Houston. My daughter's neighborhood gave us eight more fighters, and the security was built up for that neighborhood as well. My son-in-law also lacked military experience but was able to handle the security detail with no problem. Now we were rolling and had some serious momentum on our side.

Morgan told me that the project was due to get started in forty-eight hours, so I needed to get back to the camp to build our plan on how we would secure the areas after they retook them. Luckily, the new recruits we had gathered were, to a man, fresh out of the war in Afghanistan and Iraq, so their training was minimal.

Once I returned to camp, Morgan set up a planning meeting and we all laid out the resources we had to contribute in order to see how Morgan wanted to utilize them most effectively. Now we had sixty-five ex-military volunteers to secure the primary area where they would start their removal effort. I would also be actively recruiting to continue to build that number as we moved into each area.

First we would deploy troops into five strategic areas and begin the clearing. The ship channel and Refinery Row headed the list. We needed a decoy or a distraction so that all of the ISIS resources would not converge on that area from other areas, so we decided to go after an area that held little true asset value but to the Middle Eastern mind-set would make sense: we would go after a heavy concentration of the enemy districts first. By going after them it would look like we were out to snuff the uprising.

The remaining areas would be the southwest side close to the loop and the Northwest freeway corridor, after which we'd move more to the west on 290 to cover the heavily populated areas.

The areas we were not concentrating would be exposed, but actually no more than they were right now. We knew these areas were vulnerable, but we felt we could create enough of a distraction that they could hold their own. Morgan also held back a few troops in reserve in the event we needed to back up any of the security details.

Morgan said "They have a lot of resources on the north side, and it would be very visible and word would go out that we were coming in to retake the area. That way we give the impression that this is our focus without them knowing exactly what our strategy is, and we can go in under cover of darkness and take Refinery Row. Instead of our troops engaging and possibly taking a bunch of casualties we'll put up a good fight and then pull back to the north. All of our efforts must be with a lot of armor so the possibility of casualties will be small. If we use armor coming in from the north, we'd make a show, and in a stand-up fight, they'll be able to hang in there for a good stretch of time."

Morgan showed us how he would retake Refinery Row. He planned to stage troops along the beltway to prevent any additional resources from ISIS coming into the area. If the enemy took the bait and started to rally to the north side of town, he would roll all of his troops staged into Refinery Row and move all the way to the loop from the beltway. He would also air drop with choppers a couple of strike teams directly into the refineries. The plan looked good—but it was all about timing and the bad guys taking our bait.

Once we had the refinery area secured we would start the rest of the plan. The plan was to retake the business area just outside the loop in what is called the Galleria. This would stretch the enemy's resources because it would be on the other side of town. We would let it slip out to the media that it was our first target, and once we had the business area and the neighborhood secure we would start the move on downtown. Then we wait to see if they take the bait.

This would force them to keep rolling resources around the city to cover it. Our opinion was they had a lot of support from knuckleheads but they couldn't move them around very effectively to fight us. If we created the conflict we wanted on the north side and hung in there long enough to see them bring in resources, then we could pull back and move on the southwest, engage there until we see them rally resources, and then we do our actual move to retake the city from the east with an established base of operations around the critical assets on Refinery Row.

Our second phase would have the clear team in the Galleria and we would follow in two parts: First, we would have a security team establish a perimeter and put snipers on roof tops along with patrols to keep the area clear. At the same time we would work the upper middle-class neighborhoods in the area between the Galleria and the Beltway to get more volunteers.

What we did not want to have happen in the neighborhood where we're recruiting is for a conflict to start, especially before we had the business areas secured. That would've been counterproductive and would also have been a big distraction for the troops and the neighborhoods.

We knew that the ISIS group likes soft targets, so by hardening the neighborhoods we were removing soft targets quickly. We needed a conjoined effort to secure the neighborhoods while the distraction in the north was occurring. With all of the hotels in that area, if the neighborhoods became too engaged we could move people into safe zones as needed and set secure perimeters around them. Our plan was risky, but if it worked we would be securing the areas around the neighborhoods and then recruiting to reinforce the troops to allow them to move on to the next area.

However, it would not take very much to mess up the plan. If we had to clear any neighborhoods of resistance before getting the business areas secure that would slow us down considerably.

Once the refinery area was secured and the southwest business district secured, we could start moving toward the north from the southwest and the east. We knew that the northern area of town would be house-to-house suburban combat, so we were trying to save that area for last. This was the area that would see the most loss of life, both on their side and ours.

Morgan told me that he wanted us to focus on the securing of the refinery area and that we were to start pressing hard to go into every neighborhood in that area as soon as we could. It was very important that these areas be secured. The people who lived there were the ones who ran the refineries. Protecting them and their families was paramount. I knew from having worked in the plants with the hard hat types that lived in those areas that getting volunteers would not be a problem.

I started building a chart of how we would cover the neighborhoods right away. We would sweep from Highway 225 and the beltway and go north and south to each neighborhood. Our focus area would stop at I-45 south as one border and then Interstate 10 as the other. By doing this we would secure most of our critical assets and regain twenty-five percent of Houston. I told Morgan we need some help when we get close to I-45 South since that area could get dicey and he said he would be ready.

Morgan told me "Take your team and start moving into the neighborhoods closest to 225 as soon as you can get ready. In that area we will want to cover the neighborhoods before we take the assets, because once ISIS figures out what we are doing, they will come after us. We have to have a security force in the neighborhoods so they aren't vulnerable."

I thought about going into the neighborhoods in street clothes but it occurred to me that in a military uniform people were much more inclined to listen to us and to trust us. Cell phone communications were starting to come back online in many areas, as was power, so we knew that once we went in ISIS would know about it.

The areas we had already been in were keeping their generators and small cell units running, and we had built a network of secured neighborhoods by this time.

So far, those neighborhoods had not been attacked. A few had some probes enter but were quickly turned around, and some were met with gunfire. No casualties had been reported in the neighborhoods, but two terrorists had been killed.

If ISIS held true to the way they had started to assimilate Europe, they would first find pockets or areas they can control and build no-go zones: In essence, if you are not Muslim, stay out of the no-go zones. There were three areas where they were starting to build no-go zones: northeast of downtown between US 59 and I-45, south of downtown just west of I-45 in the University of Houston area and north of downtown in the Greenspoint area.

The strategy of coming in from the north with armor was brilliant: The Greenspoint area could be reinforced by ISIS from the area north of downtown by US 59 without having to get on main streets. They could use back roads and feel safer making the move. Once the armor rolled in from the north, however, chaos would break out from the 59 area all the way to Greenspoint. Our objective was to retake all areas but the three problem areas, and then do what Europe had failed to do — go into those areas and eradicate the resistance.

My team started out for the neighborhoods by 225 on Refinery Row. Once we were in the neighborhoods we found them already starting to build security measures. The recruitment had been going on since word got out what was happening in some other areas. What was so impressive was that we found another twenty-five recent military recruits and had security established around the neighborhoods in just two days. That was perfect timing because the armor was due to roll in from the north in eight hours. Now our recruitment was close to one hundred recent military troops and these guys had serious attitudes. They would fight and they knew how to fight.

We moved the recruits back to Morgan so they could get a refresher course on combat and be issued weapons. Many had weapons, only no fully automatic weapons—but ARs, AKs, shotguns, and pistols were everywhere. We had a few with long-range weapons as well.

Now you know why our forefathers had enough vision to put in the Second Amendment. It wasn't to use against the people around them: It was to defend against governments.

So far the only intervention I had seen had been from the State of Texas National Guard. The US effort seemed to be in DC and New York protecting those areas. Of course the biggest effort had to be in protecting the government that got us into this mess in the first place.

When we got back to Morgan, I was astonished. There were transport choppers and legitimate transport trucks. We had some light armor for escort, a couple of gunships to escort the choppers and the base was buzzing. There must have been five hundred troops there and they were reinforced by the hundred we had recruited. Now we had a fighting force that could make things happen.

Morgan issued the order for everyone to be ready to roll out on a moment's notice. He had reconnaissance drones up flying the target areas to make sure the decoy started working before we rolled in to Refinery Row. Just as he issued that order we got word the armor was rolling in from the north.

At first it was uneventful, but after the armor reached about a mile and half inside the beltway they started taking fire: light and from small arms, to begin with, then the thermal imagery on both the drones and the M1 Abrams starting lighting up. Groups of up to ten each were slowly making their way up behind buildings and cover to get in position.

The three tanks formed a V formation and rotated so the heaviest armor faced out. The two armored personnel carriers pulled into the V side by side for cover. Each tank was positioned to cover front and both sides. The armored troop carriers set up with their M60 and the .50 cal pointing back north along the freeway. The troops took up cover positions around the tanks. Each tank also had a .30 cal machine gun, as well as their cannons. The fire capacity of an Abrams is awesome: It carries a 105 or 120 millimeter cannon, a .50 cal machine gun, and a pair of 7.62 machine guns. Each troop carrier had six ground troops equipped with small arms.

Thermal imagery was really lighting it up now. Thermals were counting in excess of one hundred enemy combatants moving into position. Most were on the east side in the building areas, but at least thirty or so were on the west in the field and behind a restaurant. Morgan was watching the drone footage and saw four pickup trucks loaded with combatants pull out of the area close to the 59 corridor and start moving toward the Greenspoint area. He estimated another twenty or so troops were on their way. That would have the ground troops outnumbered ten to one.

Morgan ordered the drones to be ready and to target the four pickups. He would wait until he knew for sure where they were headed, and it would buy time to see if they would expose any more combatants before he took them out. He knew he had only about twenty minutes to decide. But the closer they got to the north area, the better it would be, because the combatants on the east side would not know we were watching them and not know for sure if the trucks were taken out.

As each truck was moving along they would stop and add another combatant or two to the trucks. After a few stops each one had as many as six or eight in each truck. We knew they would stop shortly and deploy the troops on foot to add to the ground numbers.

Morgan's guys in the armor were getting a little nervous. They could see the imagery and knew that forces were building up against them. They asked Morgan for orders and he said "Hold your ground, and return fire when fired upon."

And we waited.

When the trucks were within one mile of the armored group Morgan ordered the drones to fire and take out all four trucks. Watching that on thermal imagery was unbelievable. Four missiles were fired and four direct hits. Since the trucks were not at the site with the rest, the other turds were not sure what the commotion was behind them, so they stayed focused on the tanks and troop carriers. It was almost like a signal that once the trucks blew, the enemy combatants started firing on the armored group. The armored group picked groupings of personnel and returned fire, and in about one minute the numbers had been reduced to half the size they had been before.

Morgan gave the order to roll into the area they had just fired on and clear the area. One troop carrier went to the east with two tanks and one group went to the west with the other tank.

The armor rolled at such a quick pace it didn't give the enemy time to think or regroup, at 60 miles per hour and putting lead downrange in a hurry the turds scattered like quail. A few stragglers were eradicated, but the tanks kept up the pressure, chasing runners all over the area. Some ran into an apartment complex, and a perimeter was set awaiting orders on how to proceed. This looked like a roach motel; they were checking in but wouldn't check out.

Now I started to see what true urban combat was like. Lots of onlookers were standing outside to watch. They all looked innocent enough, but we all knew they could pull a gun out of their pants at any time and fire on you. Picking out the bad guys among non-combatants is extremely stressful.

We knew we didn't have the numbers to really drill down into the apartment complex so we just waiting at the perimeter to see if anything happened. Waiting to be shot at has its own brand of nerve wracking impact.

I can see why soldiers coming home from the Middle East have a huge problem with PTSD: The enemy and the noncombatants all look alike and you never know which one will shoot you. In most cases you are not allowed to shoot unless you are shot at, which means you are more expendable than they are. That is the sad reality of a war governed by politics and not concerned with victory. You can't even define what victory is if you will not define who your enemy is and focus on their eradication. But today, if you have a weapon, you are fair game.

This time, it was different, Texas had decided that regardless of what the US Government was saying we had an invasion on our own soil and the invasion had to be eradicated. If you were aiding or engaged with the enemy you would be fired upon. In essence, Texas was saying "We will take care of ourselves, and it really doesn't matter what the politicos in Washington say."

It was apparent that there would be no "I was just standing here" situations in this: Either you were for or against freedom. We had allowed too much fence-riding and political footballs for personal gain. Now there was no middle ground: You had to be for or against.

As our troops pulled up to the apartment complex, several gang banger-looking dudes came out to see what was going on. They started talking tough about how we shouldn't be there; this was where they stayed and we needed to leave. Our troops didn't say a word but trained all their weapons on them. They slowly backed off, talking trash the whole time.

Within the hour several groups came out to show a display of power and were instantly met with an announcement that they needed to disperse or they would be fired upon. They didn't leave. Another announcement was made, and they still didn't leave. Then one of them pulled a gun and pointed it at the team. That was a big mistake: All of the group died there on the spot.

From the balconies of some of the apartments our guys actually heard a cheer: It seems that lots of people who live in these complexes were as tired of the gang goons as everyone else was. Our troops stood their ground. Now we had to figure out how to separate the wheat from the chaff. So what would our approach be to moving out the innocents from the combatants?

CHAPTER 17:
RECOVERY
OR, THE END OF ALL THINGS

Morgan said it was time to roll out on Refinery Row. We saddled up, and the choppers and our armor rolled out. In fifteen minutes, our teams were over the critical areas on 225 and the beltway and the road teams rolled into position. Troops landed and dispersed, armor rolled into the target areas fifteen minutes later where they could be dispersed quickly and we gained control of the refining assets in Houston.

The plan had worked. We had no resistance in the refinery areas, and now we had a stronghold that we knew the enemy would not break. Quickly we moved the recruits that we got from the neighborhoods into position to work as a security detail, and our troops worked with them to get things settled in.

The armored group continued to clean up stragglers who fired on our teams and the group that went west eventually moved back east to set a perimeter around the HUD apartment complex where a lot of the combatants had melted away. Now with both groups working a perimeter, Morgan decided it was time to clear out the complex. By doing this, he would draw a great deal of attention to the armored team, and it would serve as our ultimate diversion. If they pulled in enough reinforcements for us to withdraw they would see that as a victory, but if they didn't we would recover some troubled areas. It was a win-win for us. He knew this would be high risk but it needed to be done so we could move on further into the area between 45 and 59.

Morgan said "I need you to go into the neighborhoods west of the 45 corridor and start to set up security teams. We know this area is largely middle class, and the transition to a secured neighborhood should be pretty easy. Still, this will be risky, so take a full security team with you."

I took two armored troop carriers with six in each vehicle, along with Torez who was now stationed at my side and had become a great friend as well. I felt totally secure with Torez and the team with me. These guys were good. I wasn't worried about how we would handle any opposition.

We rolled into the first neighborhood and things were strange. First of all, the people were really hesitant about joining us. We reached a house where the husband had been military, and he told us that the ISIS group had been in there warning all of them not to listen to what the US military was saying—they would make sure that each neighborhood was safe. What ISIS didn't say was if it was determined that anyone had worked with the military they would be executed.

So now we had to change our tactics and represent a "How do you respond to oppression?" message. We were prepared for that, but it hurt me that Americans could be subject to this kind of oppression and submit to what these scumbags said. After all, we built this country on not responding well to someone else telling us what we had to do. But the kinds of people ISIS was going after were the ones who had been trained to believe they were oppressed, and that they were not being treated right. The reality is that anyone who believes they have the right to pursue anything they want can attain it in this country. The idea of freedom has been lost and the idea of slavery has been trained into them.

(On a side note, I believe our education system had been tainted to the point that instead of seeing potential for achievement they only see what they have been told they should be given because they are the oppressed. It was a "you owe me" mentality that trained our people to just say they were owed things or retribution would be coming. Constant pounding on how our system of government is corrupt has trained all of our youth to believe a free republic form of government is the bad guy. Our educators have been telling three generations we are the problem in the world and not that we have been the solution to tyranny. Our country was built on just the opposite: If we are oppressed, we need to be free to get what we want—that is the freedom of each individual—instead of being given what we want because we feel like or have been told we were oppressed. Can you imagine how the British Empire would have responded if we said *you are oppressing us, so you owe us something?* Just look at history and you can see how they responded. It was met with a lot of gunfire. Our revolution was to remove that kind of attitude and give true freedom to individuals.

Now our generation was paying the price in blood. I couldn't believe we were standing behind weapons pointed at our own citizens and telling them we would fire if they didn't stand down, yet, here we were. Poorly educated due to our educators preaching philosophy instead of actual history, reading, writing, and arithmetic: wanting instead to preach social values to create ill-informed people who take a stand to fight against the only thing that could give them true freedom. We have been teaching how to be a nanny state and for one reason, to get votes for one party. Sadly, I have learned the party wanting votes has a Socialist agenda.)

Our team was positioned outside the apartments and just sitting and watching. Guns were trained on the complex and there were plenty of people milling around and watching what was going on. The drones were following two more additional trucks with reinforcements coming from the east. Just before they could see what happened to the other four trucks they got lit up as well. By now the body count was probably about forty combatants from the east, not counting the additional thirty or so taken out in the exchange with the armored group near I-45.

While these events were happening, the airlift continued to go perfectly. The landings had little to no resistance, and our teams were now in position guarding Refinery Row. Next step was to keep the turds bottled up and set a strong perimeter around the HUD complex near I-45.

Our drones continued to monitor the team around the apartments and keep an eye out for the enemy coming in on the flanks. Once the apartment perimeter was secured the loop would expand to take in additional neighborhoods surrounding the complex and get security teams established... or, if the reinforcements rolled to assist and our teams were in jeopardy we would pull back. Either way, we would win the day.

The security efforts we had established in the neighborhoods around Refinery Row worked perfectly. A couple of groups had tried to get in but were turned back quickly and without any exchange of gunfire. Our drones tracked the teams that confronted our teams back to where they came from and marked those areas for future reference.

The teams surrounding the apartment complex were in a tense situation. It seemed that some of the residents continued to test the boundaries of what they could get away with.

Once we had the momentum going in the neighborhoods I'd been assigned, I returned to Morgan's base camp. I updated him on the progress and so far it felt good. Morgan said that things were escalating around the country and that now the world stage was changing rapidly. Morgan said that Iran was massing troops on the Iraq and Turkmenistan border and Russia was massing troops on the border of Kazakhstan. If both moved at the same time, they would meet in Uzbekistan. Syria also had massed troops on the Iraq border and it looked like they were all positioning for a move to take Iraq and Afghanistan. If these efforts are successful then Turkey would be vulnerable.

Once these areas were secured, then an Islamic State of Iran and Syria/Russia alliance would have a powerful force to begin the march on Israel. I said to Morgan "This is setting the world stage for World War III, and with the turmoil in the US there won't be anyone to assist Israel. Hell, our current administration alienated us from them. We probably wouldn't have rallied to their aid anyway."

Under the new circumstances, I suggested to Morgan that our next major effort to retake and secure an area should be the Medical Center. I said "Houston has the best medical facilities in the world, and we will need them at the rate this thing is ramping up. How long do you think it will be before the United States is invaded?"

"We have some time but not much. We also have intelligence that South American countries including Mexico may be planning to move on the US from the southern border. Texas will be critical. If we are overrun, the US could fall. Troops deployed along the southern border have already had probes testing our ability to react. Over the last few days they have increased in numbers. The first exchange of fire happened yesterday and was met with a stiff resistance that sent them back across the river with a few casualties in tow. Arizona has been probed, California too. Arizona did pretty well, but California has been slow to react."

A dispatch came in, which he read out loud to me: "All military forces of the United States of America, be advised that a state of war now exists between the Islamic State of Iran and Syria all of their allies and the United States of America. A declaration of war has existed since 11:45 AM EST today declared on the US by ISIS and their allies.

In addition a state of martial law is being declared in the continental United States."

Morgan looked at me. "So now it begins."

"Morgan, if Russia is an ally what does that mean? Are we at war with them too?"

"What I think is that this is the end. Of all things."

Morgan called in all his senior staff for a meeting. He read the dispatch to all of them, and it was a somber moment. Morgan went on. "Not since the Civil War has a war been fought on US soil, but now that is changing. We are now to treat anyone who allies with the ISIS groups as enemy combatants. Anyone firing upon US troops is to be considered an enemy combatant. We may be killing citizens of the US, or we may be killing people from other countries, but at the end of the day we are now fighting for our homes and our families. We will be enforcing the curfew, but don't go out of your way to do these things, as we are engaged in a war, and I don't want troops being killed trying to enforce a curfew.

"Use your best judgement. Gear up. Let's do our jobs."

Morgan's team asked for any additional orders and he said "Maintain the orders we already have: That's plenty. To reinforce those orders, secure the critical assets, recruit volunteers, and retake Houston and kill any enemy combatants. This may change, but for now the threat to our freedom is the enemy within our borders, and that enemy is ISIS and any affiliates they have. We will change our tactics a little bit to secure the medical center. Those will be outlined at the appropriate time." They nodded as if to say they understood why, and Morgan dismissed them.

I asked Morgan if he had any news on the status of the military and how they were being used in the rest of the US. "The military has been running drills for several years to handle internal rebellion and most of the exercises have been focused on the gun-bearing states like Texas, Arizona and Oklahoma. Right now, their hands are full in trying to restore order and a base of government in the eastern states, but I expect their attention to turn to TAO [Texas, Arizona, and Oklahoma] soon. Our military is also gearing up, but they have no plans to go to the Middle East to fight the alliances. For now it's all about protecting and maintaining a central government in DC."

I said that I was not surprised by that, as the current administration has said all along that Muslim extremists were only one of the dangers and that the radicals in the US were just as dangerous. The sad part was that they saw conservatives as those radicals. "With only a year to go in this administration, I fully expect that when the focus turns internal and with martial law being declared we will not hold an election, and the current admin will probably stay in office for as long as they feel it is necessary. They feel like it is necessary for them to remain in power forever."

I asked Morgan "How long will it be before the local militias will be told to stand down to negotiate a settlement? Would Texas stay in the union if that happened?"

"I don't know how long, but I'd guess it'd take six weeks or so to restore order in the east, and then Texas will get a lot of political pressure to conform or be prepared to deal with military consequences from the government and the combatants. It's not my decision to make, but knowing the state of mind in Texas, secession could happen, and then we could have another civil war in the US. I'd expect Arizona and Oklahoma to join us and form a new independent country if things get really stupid."

I walked out of Morgan's office with a feeling of impending doom. Everything I had seen building up was starting to come to pass. Christians and conservatives were slowly being painted as extremists.

The government had shown a predisposition to favor the Muslim religion and distaste for Israel.

Look at the nuke negotiations with Iran, look at how ISIS was allowed to regain territory secured by US troops in Iraq, or look at the inability to push back with any strength on the incursion of Russia in independent states. Look at how the administration refuses to call acts of terror carried out by Muslims as Muslim extremists and you get the feeling that these are the last days. We are quick to prosecute a Christian organization for following their beliefs but will not condemn terror. Our country was founded on Christian principles and what we are seeing is the fundamental transformation of our country. That was exactly what was stated when the current regime took control.

So I did what any God fearing Texas man would do, I prayed and then I checked my weapons.

I imagined that once the military had order restored in the eastern US, they would start a cleanup crusade inside the US and that anyone they have deemed radicals would be rounded up.

They would start in the east and move both west and south. There would be some small pockets of resistance mostly from redneck holdouts but it would be nothing the military couldn't handle quickly.

Based on voting history it would be an easy move south through Florida and west through Michigan down to Louisiana, but Louisiana would probably call for assistance from Texas so it could quickly turn into a battleground if Texas can respond with assistance. Going into other states would be easy until they started moving more west into Wyoming: There they would have a true rural fight on their hands.

Because some states were in favor of gun control and limited the ability for their population to resist the government, we would end with a barrier that reached from Illinois down to Arkansas and that would solidify as the new United States of America.

Soon after, we would see California, Oregon, Washington, and the southern half of Colorado (which would split from the northern part and join the Union, leaving the Midwest in limbo). Indiana might resist, but they wouldn't have the resources to fight very long.

I can see how the US could be split right down the middle with Texas being the heart and soul of the independent states. Fear would probably rule the upper Midwest and all the states but Texas, Arizona, and Oklahoma would form their own union, leaving the country split into three distinct countries. TAO would be the only republic; the others either part of the Union or a democratic set of states.

I expected that the democratic states would soon join the US restructure once a fair amount of threats had been made, leaving only TAO as the lone dissenters.

But our biggest problem could be from outside forces. Once America was on the defensive and our forces were scattered and distracted, an air drop and land-based invasions would be likely. With the numbers of American troops reduced over the last seven years, we no longer have the headcount that other countries have, and we could be seen as vulnerable.

The thought of a foreign invasion gave me chills. A landing in the west would be a great strategy by our enemy and they could quickly gain the entire west coast and carve off three big states to build a base of operations. The mind-set that has taken over in those states is very passive and would bow to the invaders.

Not only would we be trying to figure out on the ground whether they are dissenting friend or true foe, now we could see troops from other countries. And if what we were seeing could come to fruition as our worst possible scenario we could see troops from the south, from Mexico and the South American coalition, as well as Russian troops from the northwest. That put at least two lines of battle on the radar not counting the internal fights to clear the cities. This looked bad.

Once a coalition from South America and Mexico would begin to mass on the border of Texas and Arizona and a coalition of states would gather in the mid-west. Texas will once again be a battleground for freedom like it was in 1836.

Of course that is my worst-case scenario. But it seems possible.

So I walked out and sat down with Torez and just stared at the ground for a while. After a half hour, he asked me if there was anything he needed to know or needed to do. I had a sort of wake-up moment and focused on him and told him the full extent of the conversation I had just had with Morgan. I also told him what I was thinking about how things would go and asked him if he thought I was off base.

Torez said "I wish you were wrong, but I am thinking you are right. So... what do we do now?"

"We'd better get busy building an army, because we are going to need one soon."

"We need one now, not soon."

I silently nodded my head: yes.

Feeling overwhelmed and underequipped, my head finally cleared and I asked Morgan if I could have a few more minutes of his time. He agreed, so I went into his office and gave him the possible sequence of events I saw coming and he said nothing.

I asked him if it came down to Texas, Arizona and Oklahoma, where the military would stand. He said "It would become us versus them, and we would have to build our own standing army as an independent republic. Frankly, the true technology edge is held in DC but we don't know how much of that will be in disarray."

"Where do you stand on this, sir? And which way will you go? Off the record of course."

Morgan paused for a long moment.

"I just hope it doesn't come to that, but if it does… Texas is my home and I will fight for it."

"That's all I need to know. You can count on me, for what it is worth, to be at your side. And to die with you, if it comes to that. Tell me, what announcement was made to the country to tell them we are in a state of war and what the real situation is?"

"Public service announcements on TV and radio started within fifteen minutes after the declaration and are being repeated every fifteen minutes. So let's get the cities recovered and then worry about how we muster forces to withstand the onslaught."

"Are any other states building a militia like we are in Texas?"

"No. They are depending on the US military and government law enforcement agencies to get it done. A few like Louisiana are pulling in the National Guard as are Oklahoma and Alabama. I would assume that within the next forty-eight hours, all of the National Guard members would be called up. The problem is that if Texas responds, how many of our guys will be called to national duty? If that happens, do we let them go or do we put ourselves in a position to rebel against the United States Government?" I waited for him to answer his own question but he didn't. I figured it would be answered if and when it happened.

I asked Morgan how many Special Forces we had available and if we could step up the recruitment by a substantial amount. Morgan said that he would have to be careful about who he selected, as they would have to be Texans, but he figured he could get a hundred or so. In the back of my mind I felt he had answered my question about what happens if the US calls up the National Guard from Texas. I asked how fast he could get them here and he said "I'll make it happen right away."

I said "I'll put together a training program and be ready for them. That would include requests for support from neighborhoods for provisions as well as make sure everyone knows about ISIS leading the surge from Mexico. We will target every neighborhood in Houston, Dallas and Austin-San Antonio for coverage within the next month. Other larger cities in Texas such as Lubbock and Amarillo as well as Harlingen, maybe even El Paso, could be covered in a couple of weeks."

I asked Morgan how much naval power and air power we would have as a republic. He said "Very little, so if we come under attack either from the coalition of states or from the South American countries—not to mention outside forces such as Russia—we would have to be prepared for beach landings and air drops when the time comes. But first we need to get our state back under control. The air power the states could bring would be a huge advantage to them, so we need to plan on building our militias so they are not easily susceptible to air attack. They need to be spread out and dug in with strategic coverage of areas.

In addition, we will need to keep the militias under the radar so they are not visible to satellite surveillance and other forms of drone reconnaissance. Ground forces would take a heavy toll on the enemy if we played it right but air power in support and possible Navy support could be rough, and there would be some from the Gulf of Mexico from both us and possibly Russian forces.

I said "The southern border will be critical once the major cities are done, so I'd like to go after them at the same time we do Lubbock, Amarillo and El Paso. That way we have more troops at the border in the event we are invaded from the south. But first when do we move on the medical center?"

Morgan said in twenty-four hours. I asked how he wanted me to support that and he said "Just keep building us an army."

"I can do that." I told Morgan my strategy for getting the remainder of the Houston neighborhoods recruited and told him how we would get our army put together, but I also told him I was worried we would be underprovisioned and underarmed.

He asked me if that was any different in 1836. I said no, but I don't want every battle to be an Alamo. I asked how Henson and the Governor were doing and what their strategy was and he said "They are trying to replicate what we are doing, but right now the flagship for the defense of Texas is us."

I told Morgan "My plan would have teams going into the neighborhoods with the recruitment effort and have small teams go into suburban neighborhood churches to spread the word. While in there, we would ask for neighborhood support for food and water. Munitions would be provided by each person carrying their own weapons and we would supplement ammo if in NATO calibers, preferably in 5.56 and 7.62 of which the ban on 5.56 has proven to be a foreshadowing of these days. Our plan would ask for volunteers and give them rally points where we could train and transport them if needed."

Morgan made good on his word. The Special Forces teams were there in a day, and we had a briefing where I went through what they should say and how things should be structured. Looking at these men and women I felt hopeful that we had a chance to make a difference, but I still had a sinking feeling we had not seen the end game yet.

The teams were rolling out within four hours of our meeting. I waited in camp with Morgan and became the go-to point in the command post for collecting information and establishing troop counts collected for the militia.

I am not good at sitting and waiting, so while I waited for the reports to start coming in I found Lopez and began to discuss the overall strategy and to pick his brain on any additional ideas he may have. When I finished I turned to Lopez and said "I'm not a trained warrior, only a warrior spirit, so what do I do?"

He listened intently, and after it was all said and I had dumped everything I knew—which took about five minutes—he turned to me but was looking beyond me and just stared for a good minute. Then he said "I may have some ideas, but let me think on it for a few and get back to you." As he walked away he turned back to me and said "I will take a warrior's spirit any day in a fire fight."

"Fair enough" I said, and we parted.

I actually went into the mess area and had something hot to eat. Once I sat down, I couldn't remember how long it had been. I do know that that forty pounds overweight thing was not an issue any more. I hadn't been at this weight since we had our first child, thirty-four years ago. All my clothes were loose, but it actually felt pretty good to have so much room to spare.

I grabbed my gear and moved close to the communications area so I could be handy if reports started coming in. While I was there, I figured that I would clean my weapons and check all of my gear. I started the breakdown of everything and got my equipment in order. It's funny how you can clean your weapon and feel better about where you are in life when you are confident they are in top condition. By doing that you knew that at least if things got bad you could at least do your part in changing it.

I went through my pack and cleaned and sharpened knives. Then I organized my pack to have the most used items on top and moved all of my winter gear to the bottom. I put my tactical shotgun on the side of the pack in a short gun case I could secure to the pack and it was quick and easy to pull. I put extra ammo for the shotgun in the top of the pack. In the side pockets I added extra ammo for the .45 and the 5.56. The pack was heavy, but it would be handy in a pinch. I kept my vest on all the time because it also provided some protection from nasty things being hurled at me at high velocity.

While I was cleaning and repacking, I started thinking of my family. I had been so engaged in getting the militia in place. I could actually see how men like the ones in the Alamo could do what they did and sacrifice as they did without being overwhelmed by the need to be with their families. It is a strange thing that drives men to do a greater good and take the focus off of the personal items. Yet I still felt like what I was doing was for them.

I knew my boys were engaged in neighborhood support efforts and that made me feel good. I felt like my wife was protected for now on the island and she most likely had some of the grandkids with her to ease the support burden for the boys. But that was all just a guess. I didn't know for sure. I decided that in the next day or two I would need to go out and figure out what was happening and make sure they were secure and in a place where I could keep an eye on them.

Once I was feeling secure and prepared, I went back in to Morgan to ask him if I could take a day or two and go check on my family. I told him how things had gone for me and how I'd had no time to prepare them, but I just needed to know they were secure and then I would be back. Morgan said that with our recruitment efforts going on, I would need to stay in communication, but he had no problem with me leaving for two days. He told me to take Lopez, a driver, and a gunner, and leave when I was ready.

I asked if I could grab an extra weapon or two, since I knew my boys were part of the neighborhood security forces, and he agreed and ordered a little additional ammo be allocated to me as well. I found Lopez. We grabbed a driver and a gunner and took one of the M60 armored vehicles and started northwest. I would go to my daughter's house first, since I knew my wife had been there earlier.

We got there without any problems and I found my daughter and her husband alone in the house. My wife had left for the island like I had asked, so I gave them the update on recruiting and how to modify the presentation. Then, after a short visit to get an update on how things were going and issuing an M4 and some ammo to my son-in-law and instruction on its use, I pulled out to go to my son's house on the north side of Houston. Rolling across from the northwest to the north side was uneventful and I arrived at my son's house about an hour and half later. He had also sent his children to Nonni's on the island and it was just him and my daughter-in-law.

My son already had a 5.56 but it was semi auto, so I left him an M4 and additional ammo. I gave him an update on his sister and told him about how to recruit in the neighborhood based on what I knew of recent events. I asked my daughter-in-law if she would like to go to the island and if my son would like to join me to help in my efforts to build a militia. I could tell my daughter-in-law was not real happy about the idea but I told her he would be safer with the Army than he would be guarding a neighborhood.

They talked about it for a while and then he said he would have wanted to go with me. I told him that was great, but he should contact his neighborhood security team and let them know he's moving to Tiki to take over a role in the neighborhood security team.

We let them gather some gear and loaded them both in the vehicle to start south to Galveston. After the introductions, I told Lopez he needed to make sure we both stayed healthy, and we started the drive.

I instructed the driver to take the long way to the island and go around to the east and come in through Alvin to the island. We made the trip with only two stops, and they were for checkpoints that had been established for security along the way.

We started rolling out, and along the way I updated my son on everything that had happened. I told him I would need a lot of help in keeping the information together and that we would be counted on to make sure there was a standing militia in Texas that would be a formidable foe. That we would not go silently into the night, and that anyone who tried to take us would pay a heavy toll. I told him about the efforts in the other cities and what our plan was for retaking Houston first, then the plan for the other cities. I told him about the global events and how they could align to be a global conflict within months. He sat quietly and listened and I could tell he was taking everything in and it was having a big impact.

After I finished with everything I could think of, I asked Lopez if he could think of anything else. He said "That about covers it, sir."

When I looked back, my son was looking out the window. He finally said "So this could be the big one, the one that ends everything as we know it."

"It could be, but if it happens it won't be without me being killed trying to change it. Look at the bright side: If this is the big one, then we know Jesus is coming back soon and things will get a lot better."

"OK. So what can I do to help?"

"First thing is spend some quality time with Mr. Lopez to learn some of the tactics we use to make sure you don't take a bullet your first day."

We pulled into the island where our local police team had a checkpoint. I showed them my island pass and they sent us on into the house. As we drove in, I noticed there was electricity. That is one of the benefits of being a small city with your own substation for power. As we turned the corner headed to the house I saw my wife and seven grandkids all out in the front yard riding bikes.

It was like being home.

As we pulled up, the kids went crazy, yelling "Mommy!" "Daddy!" "Papa!" "Uncle!" "Auntie!" and hugging everybody. This was why I was fighting: No turd is going to take this away without a life-and-death battle. I gave my wife a great big kiss and hug, and then had to hug each one of the grandkids.

After all the greetings I told my wife what was about to happen and that my daughter-in-law was going to stay there to help with the kids, and my son was going to help in the militia recruiting efforts and guarding Tiki. After the initial motherly response she said she understood.

I also gave her an M4 with three extra magazines and showed them both how to use it and to keep it handy. I placed handguns in strategic locations and told them to practice how to move around and if someone was hit what they needed to do. I told them "Trust that my son will make sure you are protected and you'll all be trained better."

I said "If the local police are overrun, we will know it and you'll have to hold out with anything you can find in the gun closet. The army will respond in an overrun situation and we will be there. It might be a good idea if you and my daughter-in-law took shifts and watch to make sure nothing crazy is happening." I left her a satellite phone she could use to call us directly if things got weird.

As we said our goodbyes I told the kids they needed to be strong and really good and to make sure Nonni and Auntie were taken care of because there were bad people running around, so be careful but know that Uncle and Papa were going to try and take care of that situation. I showed them what to do if someone was hurt and they would be the most important parts of the whole thing.

Sadly, I had to show the oldest grandkids how to shoot a pistol. What had happened to our country? I also told them we had thousands of Texas men who were doing the same thing and we would be back when things were OK.

We took the route around West Houston to get back to Morgan's camp. I watched my son as we got out of the vehicle and I started toward Morgan's tent. He followed, at a little distance. I turned to him and said "Go with Lopez and get suited up. I will see you in a few minutes: I will find you."

I walked into Morgan's tent and asked if he had a moment to talk with me he said "Absolutely."

My first words were "Hey! I don't remember those cloverleafs on your uniform!"

"Yep. That is what you call a battlefield promotion. I am now a Colonel and have this entire area of South Texas. Henson's now a General and has all of Texas."

"Congratulations. I feel safer knowing you're around."

"Oh… and, by the way, you are now a Colonel of the Texas militia."

"Thank you, but if I remember, a certain colonel of the Texas militia during the war of independence with Mexico was killed."

"It's my mission to make sure that doesn't happen this time."

I said "Thank you," and it made me feel somewhat better.

I gave him a brief on the things that had happened in the field and how well our teams were doing in recruiting. The news was very positive: We had more recruits than we had figured and our numbers were growing rapidly. I figured that once the real shooting starting we would get even more so we needed a plan to incorporate them when they came in. I told him Dallas was easy and Austin was a little rough because they all had a wait and see attitude, but surprisingly San Antonio was with us and they were building a solid resistance base. Next was Harlingen and they were moving over quickly to the militia idea once they learned that ISIS was behind the Mexican incursions.

At my best estimate we now had about thirty to thirty five thousand in our militia who were experienced military personnel and could fight, and I expected that number to grow. Not only could they fight, but in the past Texas has provided over forty percent of the military staff in the US armed forces, so we were better than ready—we were a considerable fighting force.

I asked Morgan: "How do we manage this number of troops and how do we focus them to be effective? We need training camps now, and we need to be ready to take them in and train them. Can you assign someone from the Special Forces to command areas so that each group has leadership with combat experience?" He said that would be done.

I also recommended sending at least three quarters of them to the southern border and using the remaining twenty five percent to assist in retaking the cities and establishing a secure zone in each one. I also recommended that each team get training in how to inform their family of what is going on, and how to band together for protection so each fighter felt secure for their family while taking on this mission.

He asked why we should do that. I told him my story and how it made me feel when my family was in good hands while I was fighting for them. He said he understood that and it made sense. I also said if we put three fourths of our forces on our southern border, and they were reinforced and supported by the National Guard, we may be able to hold the border—or at least make it really painful until we knew what we were facing elsewhere.

Morgan said "I'll use Special Forces to lead these teams to establish a line of defense and to establish a solid line of communications to keep us informed on the situation."

"What we should do if Louisiana calls for support? Or Oklahoma or Nevada?"

"The most important thing is to secure Texas. Once we have that established, we will render whatever aid we can to our neighbors. But our first priority is Texas; then we look elsewhere. In battle, we first accomplish our primary objective then we branch out to our secondary objective and our first objective is to secure Texas. Then we focus on spreading out to other states."

Houston, he said, was decimated. Most of the inner city had been burned and looting and murder and public executions had become the scene inside of the city. Morgan also said that ISIS was starting to establish Sharia law to establish order to the chaos. He said that to retake the city now would be a true combat scenario where we start bombing the city and reclaim what is left. I wondered if that was going to be viewed as politically correct and if we understood that to purge the problem we had to clear out the problem in its entirety and that was the solution.

Sadly, looking back at the history of the Jewish nation we see that the only time they were effective in clearing out all of the baseline resistance to their belief in God was when they removed all resistance. I remembered the book of Nehemiah in the Old Testament and started to get scared realizing what might need to be done to get things back to normal.

I suddenly realized that nothing ever changes. History just continues to repeat itself. We just continue to repeat ourselves throughout history.

Are we smart enough to see it and understand what we need to do? It is simple. Even though the times are different, the basic reason for the problems remains the same: Man is corrupt, and without God we de-evolve. It isn't like Star Trek. We are not evolving into a higher life form. Man without God is corrupt and we only get worse.

I believe in evolution, but it is *de-evolution*. We are evolving back into monkeys, and the reason they have not found the missing link is because it is in our future. I believe the reason for de-evolution is a society without God, our only stable force in an ever-changing mankind.

CHAPTER 18:
OH, CRAP

"Let me give you a brief on what has happened in the last two days," Morgan said. I reluctantly said "Okay," and realized that he had a very serious look on his face which scared me.

"First of all, the level of damage caused by the nukes has had a widespread effect on not just casualties but the general fear level in the US. Most of the people in the US are turning to the government to save them. It was determined that planes were used to pop all but two of the nukes, and they think they were the ones captured by ISIS. They were all commercial jets and we found out they have been in the states for a few months to get a routine travel pattern established.

"The one popped between Austin and Houston was at thirty four thousand feet, and the EMP and blast measured two megatons. The ones in DC and New York were about the same. Texas City appeared to be more of a suitcase nuke, less than a kiloton. We think they may have more of them and they could be hitting other cities anytime. The Federal Government declared Martial Law, and the current administration is working on clamping down on all travel and enforcing curfews all across the country. For now, the state-led National Guards are not being folded into a national effort, but we expect that to change in a few days. Should the Government assume control of all the military, most of our resources will be moved to DC to reestablish the central government. If that happens, we can just about guarantee that Texas will be overrun from the south.

"Based on how the current administration feels about Texas, they would probably be happy to see us fall. I am going to do all I can to make sure that will not happen. I believe Texas is the symbolic representation of what used to be the American spirit and we will either win or die trying—but we do have a few pockets of anarchy that must be put down, or we will fail."

That made me think of the Alamo. Texas history was the only course in junior high that I actually loved and passed with straight As.

"In the end," he continued, "we are a perfect target for invasion, so our eyes are on North Korea, China and Russia. We will have to put together our own militia and be prepared to defend not only against foreign invaders but also from our own government. Our biggest fear is the amount of funding that is needed to fight in the military environment of today. What cost the south in the Civil War was the ability to fund the military to win. Now, while I do not agree with the reason we even had the Civil War, I do agree that resources and money are what make the difference in war. Also, a big change is coming in the government: It looks like we have a new president on the way, and he is much different than what we have now."

"I am with you, and I know that the heart of Texas will live or die with the idea of *freedom or die*." I thought about the types of people I knew in Texas and what they believed in, and I knew that either we would emerge from this experience as the role model or we would die trying to live out our ideals.

Morgan said "We have now reached a point where we have Houston in a fiery inferno, and the core of the city is burned or burning, and the rest of the state is waiting to see what our action will be. My position would be go in and clear the city, and make sure the rest of the state knows we are not going to tolerate this stuff.

"As of right now, since we have teams recruiting in other cities, our first objective is to stabilize Houston and to do it quickly. However, as other cities were recruited we would build in defensive barriers to maintain and support the police in those cities."

He put his plan on the table and started out by showing the areas in the worst shape. Once he had finished his briefing, he looked at me and said "Up to this point, you have been recruiting and consulting. Now I need you and your recruits to get dirty." He pointed on the map to three areas on the north side of Houston and said he needed me to take half my recruits and clear the areas and establish secure zones.

"The objective is to squeeze them east and push them into the established perimeter we have at the beltway."

"I will do whatever you ask me to do, but I am no expert in urban warfare. I don't want to get these guys killed."

"I know that, and I'm sending with you a dozen regulars with experience in Iraq and Afghanistan who can lead the teams."

"Will we have any air support if things get really bad?"

"Yes, along with three armored vehicles.

"When do we start?" "Tonight."

I gathered the men who would lead squads of men for a meeting. I explained what we were about to do. It was met with mixed reactions. Some said they were not sure if the men were ready. Others said they were eager to get on with it.

Our first objective would be to send in recon teams to assess the situation. We needed enemy troop counts and where they were working from. I suggested civilian clothes and concealed weapons for the recon teams with established fire lines to fall back to if things get bad. We had three Special Forces guys. I turned the meeting over to them and asked them to provide instruction on how the recon should be done.

The first thing they asked for were guys who had Special Forces training. Eight raised their hands. These would be the ones we used for the recon missions. They were briefed on what to look for and how to blend in to not be obvious. Then they turned it back over to me.

I told the team leads "Once we have our recon intel, we will mount the offensive to clean the areas and establish a security perimeter. Refit with ammo and battle kits and be ready to roll out as soon as we get that information. Special Forces and the leads with SF training, please stay behind." I dismissed the others.

Lopez had had my son in tow ever since he joined up, and they had stayed with us as well. I told them they would stay with me, and our command center would be within reach of the beltway but also within reach of the areas our team was about to target. I asked the leads what they would want for support, and each said we would need to keep a team in reserve in case some heavy stuff went down.

I assigned one armored vehicle to each of the three groups. "If things get really bad," I told them, "or if you find heavy concentrations of resistance, fall back to a safe area and call in the air support. You know the fall back areas, so everyone knows where to go if needed. We have two Apaches that will be in the area and available if needed. They will provide aerial recon using their thermal and night vision. That will be handy to look for movement in the area." I checked to see if the teams had laser targeting equipment and each had been given one per area. That meant if we needed it we could also get fast movers to come in.

I asked the leads how they would approach each of the areas. They said we should lead with the armor, fan troops out in fire teams of about four per group and move through the areas. They suggested that house to house was the only way to make sure the area was clear, and that we should run parallel and no more than a block or so away if a team should get pinned down. "What we do with suspected combatants?" they asked. "If they are suspicious do we have a place to put them and a strategy for interrogation?"

That thought hadn't occurred to me so we decided to take over a high school gym as a place to keep suspects until they could be interrogated. I told them I would get with Morgan on providing intelligence staff to interview them.

Suddenly it came home to me I was about to send these men into harm's way. They also asked if we had any local police support, so that if they found resistance and they could apprehend them and they could be taken into police custody and guarded by police at the gym. I told them I would ask Morgan to get that going for us.

I asked "Could we have police support at our command post so we could dispatch them to pick up fighters or suspects and take them into custody? Once we start moving into the area and things become more secure, we can move the police presence up to the security teams for faster access to the strike forces."

I also suggested that we as we push through we leave behind small fire teams as security to make sure combatants don't duck out of site and then catch us from behind. They all agreed that would be necessary. I asked if we had enough snipers to provide oversight with the teams, they said they did and they would make sure that happens.

I assigned all of the teams to one of the SF trained members, so each team had experience and combat tactics available. I asked the leads to find for each fire team someone who has leadership experience; at a minimum, a corporal. "If there are not enough to go around," I said, "we will need to make bigger teams." My biggest concern was getting everyone back alive. But it made sense we should keep the teams to four or five so we could cover more area.

I dismissed them to go get their teams ready to fight.

That night we pulled out in a convoy with fifteen vehicles in it. We moved around the belt because we knew our guys had control of it. One armored vehicle was in front, one was in the middle, and one was in the back, with twelve transports, making nearly two hundred men. Lopez and I rode in the first armored vehicle and my son was in the first transport. We were spaced about five car lengths apart while on the freeway. Our destination was an office building that I knew had available empty space, as my office had just moved out of there and they were having trouble getting renters. It was one block from the beltway and directly facing I-45.

We figured the worst area would be the HUD apartments within a mile of the freeway. There were at least three complexes. We figured if we cleared them first, we could use more troops, and once the biggest trouble spots were cleared we could fan out with a lower risk level.

Having been in these complexes before, I knew there was a possibility of reinforcements coming from the east. We asked the Apaches to hang out in that area to watch our backs and they would still be close enough we could call them in if we needed to.

Forty minutes later, we pulled into the office building and pulled the vehicles in the covered parking area so they were out of sight. We positioned spotters and two sniper teams on the roof with a 360 degree view and placed security fire teams around the garage.

Once it got dark, we sent recon teams into the neighborhoods to get a status. We also kept a lights-out scenario in the office building so it was not apparent there were people inside. Five loosely formed teams of three men each made their way out to check the surrounding areas. We had a couple of civilian vehicles that joined us about dark and we loaded teams in them to be dropped on the edges of areas we wanted to recon. Each team had a radio and was equipped with small concealed arms easily hidden in clothing. No backpacks or other obvious military items would be used. We recruited mostly Hispanic and Black team members to make the recon missions. Their orders were not to engage unless lives were in jeopardy.

The teams were instructed to report back by 5 AM so they would not be out during the daylight hours. An additional directive was to locate good sniping areas for overwatch while teams were going in to clear their designated areas. The tricky part was to make sure local police knew that, if they came across any of our people not to arrest them. That was a communications challenge, but somehow it worked out. Only one team was stopped, and they were quickly released.

Our teams were spread out on a few of the floors in the office building getting some sleep and rotating their watch duties. Keeping two hundred men quiet and still is a challenge, but these men were awesome. They seemed to understand the gravity of what we were about to have to do. We positioned additional spotters on the ground floor, the third floor, and the top floor—where Command was—to keep more eyes on the surroundings. We put a fire team of three in the main floor reception area with instructions to be still, hidden and lights-out.

We had just enough night-vision equipment to cover all of the critical areas, plus a few extras. We would need these once the fighting began, but for now they were to be used to watch over the position.

I called a team lead meeting in an interior room of the building where lights would not be seen. Our objective was to plan and plan again on how we would move through these areas. Until the recon teams came back in, we only had theories about what we would do. At 2:30 AM we decided to get a little sleep until the recon teams started coming in.

Thank God for war experienced veterans: They know how things need to operate. If it had been up to me, I probably would have just led the teams into the housing and gotten a bunch of them killed. Not to mention that we would have had a lot of collateral damage in civilian lives lost in the process.

But as the teams started showing up, the recon they collected was absolutely invaluable. The first team reported that the activity seemed to slow down about 3 AM and most began to turn in for the night. They designated several hot spots where they believed most of the activity was based. The best part was that they were not acting as paramilitary units, but as thugs, and they trolled the streets as groups of punks until 2:30 then went back to the place they were staying and went to bed.

They also noted they started drinking about 11:00 PM and most were pretty tipsy by about 1:30 or so. That also meant they were not up at the crack of dawn either. So as the intel rolled in we started building a plan to have the locations defined and for our teams to roll in starting at 5 AM and ending at 9 AM. That way before the rest of the civilians started waking up, we had removed insurgents.

With silenced weapons and overwhelming firepower we could start taking these areas quickly—Now, that would work for a day or maybe two, and then we would have to revisit our plan, but if we targeted the biggest areas first, we would have limited resistance when we moved in during daylight hours in the following days. By our calculations we figured about five days to retake our areas assigned.

I updated Morgan on what we found and told him we needed to rule the night and have solid recon before the action to make sure we had solid targets. He agreed and sent out the order to all teams working in effected areas to use the same plan of attack. Thermal imagery and constant night vision helped us build trend analysis of how the movements were proceeding and what the housing elements held as far as personnel.

After taking an area, we needed a plan for police to pick up turds and for weapons stashes to be picked up and destroyed. Once they were in police custody we had to depend on the fact they had a place to keep them all and to interrogate them for their involvement. One thing I have learned is that people are expert liars; they will tell you they are the victims when they have been the perpetrators.

One other thing we would attempt to collect is gathering all but a single firearm from the housing unit individuals so that there would not be any supply going out. We did not want to restrict the right to bear arms for civilians. Each civilian must be entitled to a firearm for their own personal protection. Later, that would prove to be a good decision.

In addition we wanted the Apaches to monitor all vehicle traffic in and out of the area to start building some intel. We added drones to watch traffic movements and build some patterns.

The next night we decided to roll out. We had locations of turd piles, and were going after those first.

As soon as the sun started setting to our backs in the west we started our fire teams out and had all local police on alert to stand by for our calls. The first targets we had designated went down with very little resistance. As we expected, each group said they were not doing anything, so now we had to have PD take them back and show them the intel tapes we had showing otherwise. We made amazing progress until about 2:00 AM, and then we hit a roadblock. Literally, the group we had targeted had built a fortification to prevent our teams from entry, so now it was apparent they had communications within the groups, and we assigned comms guys to figure out how they were talking.

Now we had a problem, instead of just rousting turds and getting them into custody we had to break the barriers and take them by force. We had hoped this would not be the case, but we were prepared for it. We deployed fire teams and brought in the armor to stand in front to openly challenge the blockades. This was a little bit harrying for a while until we found out whether or not they had any heavy weapons. As it turned out they did have RPGs but our overwatch snipers took them out as soon as they stood up to shoot. After the first two went down trying to use them, they stopped reaching for the RPGs.

Now we were at a standoff. They stood behind cover and fired a few shots in our direction but it was all small arms and there were no casualties.

We announced that if they didn't surrender their arms and walk out with their hands up, we would return fire. I watched as they discussed it and then they opened up on us. Our team returned an overwhelming volume of fire. They lost four fighters, and then their firing ceased. They threw down their arms and walked out. Seems that they figured their cause was not worth dying for after all. But just as we thought it was going to be resolved a group of three started firing at us and it was clear they were not going to stop until either we were dead, or they were. So we obliged them: The three were dead in seconds by return fire from armor and troops.

OK. That was resolved.

We returned to base with twenty-three people arrested for criminal intent and terroristic acts. We left a team on watch to keep the area under control, so we didn't lose ground we had already recovered.

Once back at base, we debriefed on what happened and how we should adjust our next confrontation.

One thing you learn is that "it only works once," then you need a new twist each time after that, so the next night, we decided to move later: Our move would be at 2:00 AM, and we would target a smaller, much more populated area.

Intel showed that there was a concentration where as many as twenty fighters were operating from one location. This time we decided to use an Apache and take it out once we were in support areas to pick up any stragglers that may want to leave.

Thermal imagery determined there were at least fifteen of them in there. We launched two missiles into the house. There were no survivors in the house. Our teams picked up three running out of the area and they are were taken into custody.

After this series of events, I updated Morgan on our progress. He seemed pleased, but a little detached. I asked him if we were on plan and he said "You guys are doing fine." Then he said "California, Washington State and Oregon have formed their own state and are trying to align with Canada." He was clearly angry that when the defecation hit the rotary oscillator the liberal states bailed and went somewhere else. He didn't like the fact the union was breaking up. I didn't like it either, but honestly I felt like they hadn't been part of the union that was America for some time.

He reminded me that for now we had to focus on securing a line from Mexico coming into Texas, and get the cities cleared of problems. So I asked him "Are you OK with the team leads finishing up our assigned areas and for me to go to the border and start recruiting there to get our line solidified?"

"It makes sense, and we need to cover our back door. How about if you form a team and head south, starting in Matamoros?"

I called up the usual list of suspects, starting with Lopez. I asked him to select a group of specialized Spanish speakers and join me in our meeting room.

Lopez found a crew of five to accompany us. We sat down, and I told him what we were going to do. His first question was "How will we pay them?"

"Excuse me? I am not sure what you mean."

"Well, if the US had been serious about border security they would have paid the ones living down there to be the security force and keep everyone else out."

"Well, now, that is interesting. You mean we commission the ones that are living there to defend the border and pay them and they will do it?"

"Absolutely. The reason they are here is to support their family and themselves and they don't care what the job is."

"So we have had our border security here all along but we would rather spend billions on political agendas when we could have secured our border a long time ago?"

"Absolutely."

I told them "Get a plan together to start the recruitment effort. I am going to talk to Morgan and the Governor."

CHAPTER 19:
IT WAS HERE THE WHOLE TIME

I called Morgan and told him Lopez's idea. I could hear his brain crunching the idea, like gears turning.

At first he was thinking I was an idiot. "Texas may not have the money to pay them for this action, what do we do then?"

"Well, if we were to break out of the US government agreements and form a true republic again like we said we were thinking about, we could take back Texas. I know breaking from the Union doesn't sit well with either of us but, maybe we could just take back Texas real estate and this could be our chance to save the Union we both believe in. If Texas could take the lead in building a strong state that wants to build and become a part of the new Union as well as lead the way for the others we may have a chance to save our country."

"Okay, saying we pitch this to our governor, how do we pay these people?"

"We do what the British did in the 1600s and promise that for every man who fights, we give them property to homestead. My grandfather came over as a bond slave, but after ten years he was designated a free man and received one whole acre for his homestead. Also, if a man is killed in action defending Texas, we will award his family the property. Let's take some of the allocated government and state lands and say that if they will fight and secure our borders, we will give them property where they can build a new life."

"There is no way I could even start down this trail unless the Governor is on board."

"You got that right. We need to set up another meeting with him."

Morgan had me meet him at his HQ and we would go to the Governor to present our crazy idea. I had no clue how Morgan had presented the idea and why the Governor agreed to meet. I ran through every possible scenario in my mind to prepare.

I met up with Morgan and we started the drive to the Governor's mansion for the meeting. I was not prepared for the response from our Governor. We walked in, and he got up and walked over to us and shook our hands and said "I'm really glad you are here. I understand you have some ideas on how we can secure our state? I want hear all about it."

First of all I was set back with his genuine attitude of wanting to hear our proposal, so I started with the facts of how the idea was presented to me by Lopez and how I came to the conclusion I did.

He looked at both of us and said "Let's make it happen."

I was in shock. I expected more of a battle, but he looked at me and said "I studied history in school too, I know how the country was founded. This makes a lot of sense. I studied Texas history and I know we have the heart and the foundation to rebuild our country and make it right again."

I asked him "When we were looking at declaring Texas a republic?"

"We are within a week or two." He showed us a map of property that could be allocated to defenders of the Republic. He promised he would sign a declaration stating that, as our policy, each person would get five acres of land if they fought for Texas.

I left his office with a feeling of purpose and that we now had something that would win the hearts of each Texan. They would now have skin in the game. We could win this. But how to get the message out without being killed in the process?

We pulled out in a convoy of four vehicles, all armored for light weapons: two with M60s and one with a 50 cal. My son was in the third vehicle. In each vehicle were four troops. I was in the second vehicle with Lopez as my driver. In the lead vehicle was a special ops sergeant and three privates. In the vehicle behind us two special ops personnel and two privates. The last vehicle had two more special ops and two privates. We were headed south along highway 59 and for the first two hours of the trip it was really quiet and we didn't have any trouble.

As we crossed into Victoria we noticed something wasn't right. The streets were empty. Not even the usual wanderers and curiosity seekers were out, and it was only 8:00 PM, but if no one was shooting at us we were good, so we kept driving.

We had just cleared the loop around Victoria headed south when things went bad. Evidently word had gotten out that Texas was trying to recruit citizens to fight and ISIS, the Cartels and the Black Panthers had set up a trap just for us. As usual, if you make plans and there are lots of people involved, someone says something to someone else and before you know it everyone knows what the plan is.

As we started south on Highway 59 out of Victoria I was looking back to the North and saw a red glow coming from San Antonio and Austin. If you looked behind us, even though it was 120 miles, you could still see the skyline above Houston, glowing orange. When I looked back ahead the vehicle in front exploded. I remembered seeing a streak of light coming from the right side, and then everything blew up in front of us. We pulled over to the left side of the road and used the damaged vehicle as a cover point.

We disembarked and were setting up in cover positions around our vehicle. Our gunner was starting to light up the areas where the flashes were coming from, but just as we started really laying down some cover fire, another streak of light came directly at our vehicle.

Lopez shouted "RPG, cover!" and we all dove into the ditch on the side of the road. I was a lot slower than the young men, and before I could get down, I was hit by the explosion.

Searing heat, burning pain in one arm and a leg. It knocked me about ten feet. I landed hard and awkward. For the first moments after the blast my ears were ringing so badly, I couldn't hear anything else. I tried to do a health check but things just didn't seem to work on my body. I rolled on my back but couldn't use my arms very well.

Within seconds Lopez was over me and I could faintly hear him telling me to stay still and to stay with him, but I was fading. I could taste copper and smell things burning. I felt like I was going to slip away, and for now it seemed fine. I was content with going away. I made peace with God a long time ago and was ready for eternity.

As I slipped into blackness I was ready to meet my maker. I was frustrated I had not completed my tasks. I thought about my family and what would happen to them. I asked Lopez about my son, he said he was good. Then it went dark.

Sometimes stuff just happens.

CHAPTER 20:
THE END OF THE BEGINNING

I started fading back in and realized I was on a medevac chopper going somewhere.

I could feel the beat of the blades in my chest... or that could be lingering effects from the blast concussion. My ears still rang, but that could be the whine of the engine. I had an IV in my arm and a medic was patching holes in several places.

The medic said "Welcome back."

"It's good to be back," just as Lopez and my son appeared over me. He asked me how I felt and I said "It feels like I've gone to a turkey shoot, and I was the guest turkey."

He grinned. "Well it looks like you are going to be OK. You will be taking it easy for a while since your arm, one leg and a few areas in your behind may be sore. You may not be able to pass through a metal detector at the airport."

"Lopez, did we take any casualties?"

"One soldier died in the lead vehicle, three more are in the hospital and there's you. Once the Apache showed up, things got real loud and then quiet in a hurry."

"We were still on track to get to south Texas?"

"Our teams are down there right now. Looks like the response is going really well. We don't have a headcount of volunteers yet but it's promising." Lopez looked at me. "The last thing you said before you passed out was what difference had you made, you asked if you had been significant. My guess is we are just getting started and it wouldn't be the same without you. After all, how would I fully utilize my training if I didn't have you to monitor? Even my medical training is getting a good workout. Besides, it was fascinating watching you fly over me like Superman when the RPG hit the vehicle. But I don't remember Superman yelling like that."

Lopez handed me my wallet. It had a shrapnel hole in it

"Well that figures. My wallet had holes in it before all this started, and now it's official. This isn't a physical war, it's a spiritual battle."

Then I went back to sleep.